I0699714

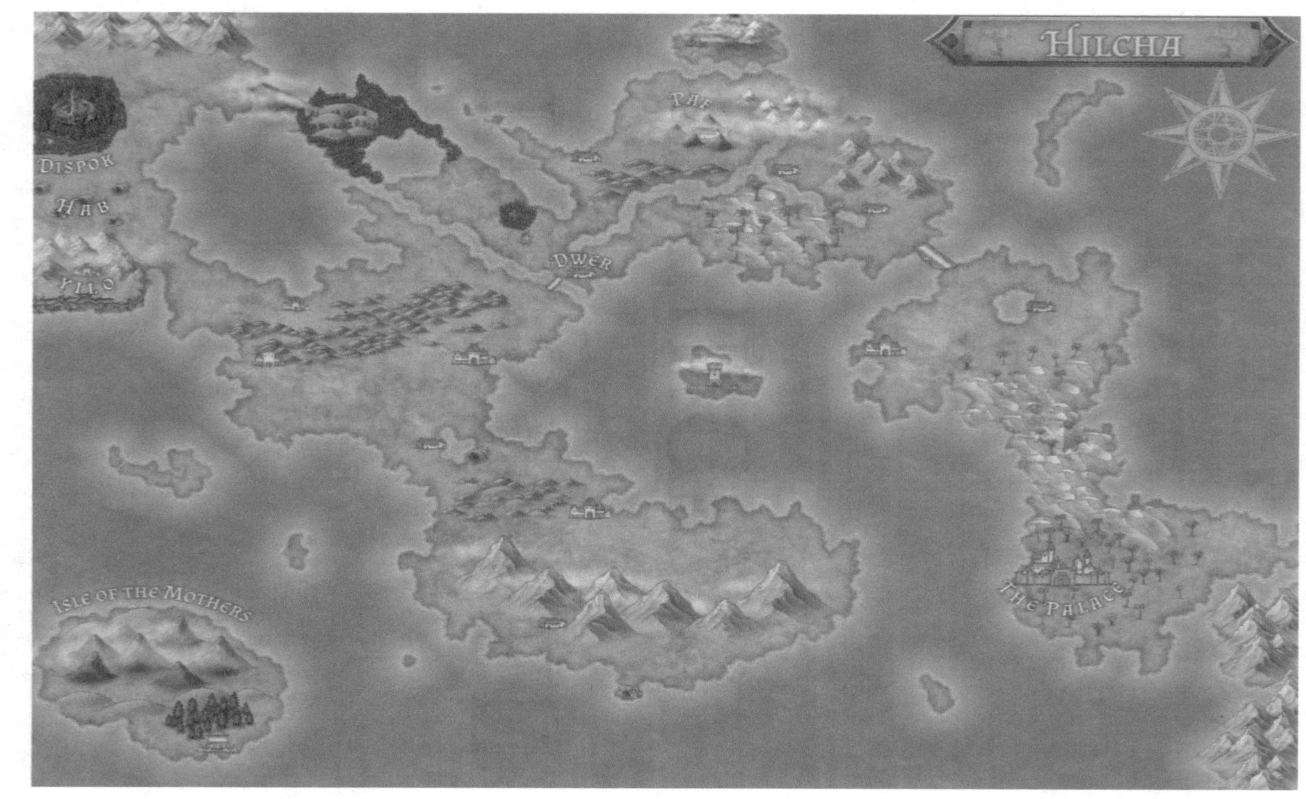

HILCHA
DISPOK
HAB
YILO
DWER
PAE
ISLE OF THE MOTHERS
THE PALACE

THE STOLEN

PRINCESS

A KUIN OF HILCHA

ADVENTURE

*For my beloved children,
and every child that has ever
dreamed of another world.*

E-book ISBN: 979-8-9858505-3-6
Print ISBN: 979-8-9858505-4-3

Copyright © 2024 by Pettibone Fuerst Publishing

All rights reserved.

No portion of this book may be reproduced in any form without written permission from the publisher or author, except for short excerpts used in review or as permitted by U.S. copyright law.

Cover design by Rena of Blackstone Book Cover Design
Map created with Inkarnate
Language of Hilcha created with Vulgarlang

Prologue

The boy and the girl lay unconscious on the table in the middle of a large chamber. Dark smoke swirled around them, unnatural black flames burning on torches throughout the room.

"They must remember nothing," a voice hissed from the smoke.

"They will not. What shall we put in their minds instead," a second voice asked, one that sounded like an ancient woman with sandpaper for vocal cords.

"Leave the girl blank. Let her lack of memory haunt her. The boy, give him memories of a family. A happy family. And then take that family away. Kill them and leave him alone in the world."

If smoke could smile, the second voice would be grinning as it answered. "Excellent, B'nakma."

The smoke that swirled around the two children began to envelop them. Soon the two breathed it in, and with it the darkness that swallowed their memories, their very selves.

The form of something near a person materialized and spoke with the first voice. "Take them to another world. Make sure that they survive. I will need them again, but for now they are far too dangerous to us here."

Two ancient looking crones appeared, one behind each child. "Yes, B'nakma," they said in unison.

Scooping up the children, they walked forward. "Dfîk ta byînyig fî hya kse bre kpe pî." *Open and take us where we need to go.*

A round portal appeared on the ground before them. The two old women stepped into the portal, and before either they or B'nakma knew what was happening, a white cat leapt in after them.

B'nakma tried to grab the cat and was certain that the hand he formed had scratched its head, but the portal closed and B'nakma was left alone before he released the frail form that he had taken, and the room was empty.

1

Kuin sat straight up in her small, twin-size bed. The light from the streetlamps outside her window cast shadows across her floor. She took a moment to focus herself, to accept that it was just a dream and that she was in her room and not in the clutches of that smoke demon that she'd dreamt about her whole life.

She glanced around her little room, her clothes sat neatly folded on the small table under her window, her clock sat on the floor next to her mattress, which also lay on the floor. The book she was currently reading rested next to her on the pillow. She didn't have much: a warm room, an old twin-size mattress, a few changes of clothes, and a roof over her head.

Her heartbeat slowed to normal as she took mental inventory of her belongings and surroundings. She wasn't in that dark, smoky chamber watching as those creatures again took the two children away. She really needed to stop reading fantasy novels before she went to sleep, but they were her escape from an otherwise depressing existence.

She didn't have parents. Well, obviously she came from somewhere and had parents in the biological sense. But she didn't know who they were, she couldn't remember them at all. She had spent her life bouncing from foster home to foster home; some much better than others, but none of them actually *home*.

When she turned twelve, she ran away from the foster home that she was in at the time, the 'father' of the house was mean and a bit creepy. She had had enough and decided that she would be better off on her own. She had taken the money that they hid in the old coffee can in the cupboard, almost two hundred dollars, gotten on a bus from Detroit, Michigan to Cleveland, Ohio. From there she had ended up in Lorain.

It was late summer when she had arrived in Lorain, Ohio, and she had managed to spend her first few weeks sleeping hidden on Lakeview Beach, or on the rocks at the Mile Long Pier. She stole food from gas stations as the last of the money she had taken ran out.

That was when Kuin met Belly. Belly had caught her trying to steal his watch, she had in fact stolen his watch, but instead of confronting her, he let her think that she had successfully taken the piece of jewelry without him knowing. Fifteen minutes later, as she settled in to where she had her few belongings stashed under a blanket she had found in a dumpster, a hand had grabbed her by her hair.

"Care to earn a better place to sleep, or shall I just give you a good beating for taking my watch," his oddly high-pitched voice had asked.

The man was just under six feet tall, but he was large, his stomach no doubt earning him his name. Kuin would have expected him to have a deep, powerful voice, but when he spoke she had to stifle a laugh because all she could think of was some sort of character from a Jim Henson show.

"I'm listening," she had said through gritted teeth, "though I'll be able to pay attention better if you let go of my hair."

An hour later, she was sleeping in a dusty corner in the basement of the Palace Theatre, one of six kids sharing the space. Belly's terms had been straight forward: bring him at least a thousand dollars' worth of jewelry, electronics, or really anything of value, every month, and she would have a warm place to sleep, with food and a shower. It was certainly better than sleeping tucked in on the rocks along the shore of Lake Erie, and it saved her from whatever he would have done had she not accepted his offer.

That had been two years ago. In the time between then and now, she had earned not only her place in his group, but a small room above the theatre; just as dusty, just as dreary, but hers alone with no one else to bother her.

She was so good at stealing that she had managed to stay at least a month ahead with Belly for the last year. Currently, she had two months paid in advance. This meant that she had time to do other things than just steal and survive. She would go to the library, just a couple of blocks away, and read.

Initially she had planned on reading only non-fiction, educating herself as best she could given her lack of a standard education. But one day, she had found the fantasy section, and books by the likes of James Islington, Fiona McIntosh, Victoria Schwab, and of course her favorite, J. R. R. Tolkien. Once she found their worlds, found that she could escape into a life of adventure, magic, and faraway places, her life became a little more bearable. Even if it was only temporary, the escape from her reality had helped her to find a happiness that she had not known before then.

Sometimes she would take one of the books with her to the beach, often sneaking onto the private beach behind the Myeb, a long-closed Mexican restaurant on the shore of Lake Erie. The building was shaped like a castle, its edifice reminding her of something from one of her novels. She would imagine as she snuck across the property that it was a real castle, that inside were knights, a king and queen, maybe even a sorcerer.

But she would only think of that until she reached the back of the property and made her way down onto the small beach. No one ever found her there. She had heard Belly say one time that the building next to it was once a fast-food restaurant, and that it had been open to the beach for patrons, but that was long before her life.

Her thoughts were snapped back to her room by a knock on her door.

"Kuin, you up? It's time to get to work," a boy's voice called through the door.

Her best friend, Graystone, always looking over her, always helping her to survive. If she felt like she had any family in the world, she knew it would be him.

"Yeah, I'm getting up."

"Okay," the boy said, "then I'm heading out. Probably going to head toward the west side. I'll see you in a few hours."

As she moved down the quiet street, Kuin knew that the man in front of her was oblivious to her existence. The man had his head down, eyes buried in his phone. There was light snow falling and the sound of their footsteps was muffled by the wet cover. It wasn't particularly cold yet, but with two weeks until Christmas it was at least cold enough for a sticky snow. Kuin hated snow, and she hated cold, and she hated winter. Except for right now. For the next few weeks, she was grateful for the snow. Christmas was her favorite holiday, and she loved when there was snow for it. She didn't know why she loved Christmas so much, it wasn't like she had ever had the feeling of waking up and running to the tree to open her gifts. She had no family to celebrate the holiday with, and she had never had a home to have a tree in.

But she did have Graystone. He was her best friend, and the only one that ever actually cared about her. He would always tell her what it was like to celebrate with family, to wake up and open gifts, to have dinner with all of the people closest to you. He had a family once, before the accident. His parents had loved him, had taken care of him and given him a wonderful childhood. Until the day that they were going on one of their weekend adventures. He always says that he can't remember the accident, amnesia from the trauma the doctors say, but he remembers waking up in the hospital. Their car had been hit by a truck, the driver drunk and apparently unable to see the red light that he should have stopped at. One minute they were on the way to a new National Park for the weekend, and the next he was waking up alone in a hospital bed three states away from home.

The man in front of Kuin stopped suddenly, mumbling some curse at his phone and snapping her back to the task at hand. She ducked behind one of the parked cars and looked to make sure that no one else had come onto the street while her mind had wandered. It was empty of sound and footprints, save the sound of the man still muttering and the footprints that he had left. Her prints fell perfectly into his, and even if he bothered to turn around he would see only his own. Unless of course he happened to notice the two prints that she made when she took cover behind the car. But those were at least twenty feet behind him, and he had no idea that she was even following him. Still, she realized that she needed to be more focused. Letting her mind wander would do nothing but get her caught; and the last thing she needed was to get caught.

She was only fourteen after all, and if she were to be caught she would end up in a group home somewhere with people that would do God knows what to her. At least that's what Belly always tells her. Belly, most certainly a name that he adopted for the girth of his stomach and not one given him by the devils that spawned him, was a miserable man. He ran a little ring of pickpockets, a bunch of underage kids with nowhere else to go that somehow ended up with him. He was not a nice man, though not cruel either. He gave them a warm hideout, food that was not great but at least edible, and he made sure that no one from any other gang messed with them. But he also was fond of hitting or kicking them when his temper flared, and it flared a lot. He never beat them, not to the point of injury at least. He just reminded them that he was bigger and he was in control. As long as they stayed out of his hair and brought him their due every month, he left them alone.

The man shoved his phone in his back pocket, and she saw the glitter of the watch that had caught her attention earlier. She also noted what looked like a diamond ring glistening briefly in the streetlight before he shoved his hands in his coat pockets and started walking again. He was moving faster now, not too fast, but certainly walking with a purpose. She fell back in step and followed him. For a block and a half she carefully closed the distance until she was only a few feet behind him. She was just about to bump into him when someone bumped into her first, knocking her into the snow.

"Oh, I'm sorry miss," a deep voice purred, and the man she had been following looked back briefly before marching away even faster.

"What the hell," she said as she looked up at the man that had knocked her over. He was tall, at least six feet, if not a few inches extra. He wore a perfectly fitted white suit, and an expensive looking charcoal winter jacket. His hair was as white as the fresh snow that was falling, all except one patch of black on his left temple. But it was his eyes that drew in all of her attention. His right eye was cerulean, while his left eye was bright yellow, almost golden. She had never seen anyone with mismatched eyes, nor had she ever seen eyes that were golden.

"I hadn't noticed you there," he said, extending his hand.

Kuin ignored it and stood. "Well maybe you should be more observant," she snapped. This man had just cost her this week's due, and probably a little extra. Extra was good at this time of year, because she always got something for Graystone for Christmas.

"I assumed you were trying to go unnoticed," he said with a smirk. "Or were you simply trying to go unnoticed by the man with the nice watch?"

Kuin feigned ignorance. "I was just trying to walk home, and now I get to do so with wet clothes thanks to you. If you'll excuse me," she said, brushing past the man.

He grabbed her wrist as she went past, and twisted it. Kuin let out a yelp of pain. "What is wrong with you?"

When he twisted her wrist just a little more, his wallet fell to the ground from her other hand. "Clumsy me," he said lightly. "I guess I do need to be more observant."

Kuin wrenched her arm free and ran. She cut expertly down side streets and alleys, though she could tell immediately that the man had not pursued her. The only footsteps had been her own.

Graystone tore off a piece of his roll and handed it to Kuin as she told him about the man that foiled her grab. They were sitting on opposite ends of her small mattress. "So he not only stopped you from snagging the watch and ring off of your guy, but he felt you, of all people, lift his wallet," he asked through a mouthful of stew and bread.

"Yeah and it was like he just wanted to stop me. He didn't follow me, he didn't try to take anything from me, he just stopped me from getting what I needed to pay Belly."

Graystone cocked his head to the side as he chewed. Her sandy hair was pulled into a frizzy ponytail, the , and she looked like she could use a shower. The best that she could hope for was a cold bath. "Well at least you're paid up for a while yet."

He was right of course. She had a couple of months or so before she would owe Belly anything. She was good at lifting valuable items, and she always stayed ahead on room and board. But it hadn't always been like that, and the thought made her shudder.

"You know I don't like to get too close to my deadline. Before you got here…" her voice trailed off. If not for Graystone helping her get ahead, she would never have survived. He had shown up around a month after she arrived. She was eleven at the time, and he was fourteen. She remembered how much older he seemed to her then. He showed up at the theatre one night, his caramel skin covered in dirt and his hair a big, knotted mess. He convinced Belly to let him stay for the night, and since then he has paid his dues on time.

"But I'm here," he said, snapping her back to the now, "and I'm not going anywhere."

Kuin ripped off a small piece of her bread and dipped it in the stew. It didn't taste horrible, but neither does cardboard. It would at least stop her grumbling stomach. "But you won't be for long."

Graystone sighed dramatically. The boy was almost a man, seventeen and a half, and soon he would be able to live on his own. "We will be together," he said with a roll of his eyes. "You know that I'm not going to just leave and not make sure that you can come with me. We'll figure it out."

Tears pricked at the corner of Kuin's eyes. She ran her hand through her hair, hoping that Graystone wouldn't notice her brushing her sleeve over her tears as she did. "I know, but I'm not going to hold you down. You'll be eighteen, you'll be able to go anywhere. I'll still only be fourteen. I can't get a job, I can't go to school, and if I get caught living with you, I will be taken and put in the system."

Graystone set the stew down on her table and moved beside her. "We'll figure it out," he repeated. "You're my best friend, at this point you're the only family I have. I won't go anywhere without you, and I won't let anyone take you away."

Kuin laid her head on his shoulder. From the beginning he had been like family to her. "D'nu," she said. The word had meant 'family' to her for as long as she could remember. She couldn't really explain it, but there were some things that in her head had a different word attached to them. It was as if English was not her native language, even though it was the only one she knew. The only person that she had ever told that to was Graystone.

"D'nu," he repeated. "Always."

2

Kuin woke up just as the sun was setting. After the sun set was her favorite time to operate, and she needed a good night if she was going to make up for coming back empty handed this morning. The man's face flashed in her mind, his strange but beautiful eyes and his pure white hair. It still upset her that she was foiled, but more so that he felt her grab his wallet. That never happened to her. In almost four years doing this, she had never been caught.

She looked out of the small window in the attic and smiled. The colors of the sunset were muted by the clouds. If she was lucky, it would snow again.

She pulled on her sweatpants and hoodie and left the house. She walked around downtown, slowly observing those around her. Typically, there wouldn't be anyone in this neighborhood that she would steal from. She only stole from folks that looked like they could afford to replace the items, and people around here didn't fit that description. The streets were nearly empty, the snow starting to fall probably keeping most people home. Hopefully downtown wouldn't be slow. Her phone buzzed in her hoodie pocket.

I got caught by a guy. I got away but sirens everywhere and idk if they'll find me.

Graystone's text sent her heart rate sky high. **Just left the house, where r u?**

She headed towards the west side, he probably had done the same. She walked for what felt like forever, the lights of downtown fading slowly behind her. He still hadn't responded.

Her phone vibrated again. **I'm fine, don't come. I'll see you at the theatre.**

Like hell, she thought. He must have gone west, right? She kept walking, but without knowing where he was she knew it was a waste of time to try to find him.

Things had been quiet for a couple of minutes, and Graystone knew he had to move. He slipped out from behind the dumpster and was immediately face to face with a cop.

"Drop the gun," the cop yelled as he shined his light into Graystone's face and drew his weapon.

Graystone was confused, scared, and couldn't think fast enough. He glanced at the phone in his hand. "It's my phone," he said, holding it out for the cop to see. All the cop saw was something black being pointed at him, and he fired three rounds center mass.

Kuin's stomach and chest burned with the most intense pain that she had ever felt. She screamed out and collapsed to the ground, clutching herself.

"Are you okay," a woman's voice asked.

Kuin looked up to see a woman with nice clothes and plenty of jewelry heading directly towards her. The intensity of the pain was gone, but it left a dull burn behind.

"She's fine," a man's voice answered. "Just getting her first period, she texted me and thankfully I was close by to pick her up."

Holy crap, it was the white haired man. He had just pulled up in a brand new Mercedes. "Are you her father," the young woman asked skeptically before Kuin could say anything.

White haired guy shook his head. "Uncle," he said, reaching down to help Kuin up. "Isn't that right Kuin?"

She took his hand. How did he know her name? Holy crap, had he been following her? "I…umm…yeah, right."

The woman still didn't seem convinced. "Are you sure you're okay honey?"

Kuin straightened a bit. "Yes, I'm fine, thank you so much. I'm sorry to have worried you."

The woman smiled and seemed to relax a bit. "It's fine, don't worry about it. I remember the first time that pain hit. You just go home and let your uncle take care of you."

When the woman had turned and walked away, Kuin yanked her hand from the man's. "Who the hell are you?"

The man studied her for a moment. "My name is Robert Steekus, you do not need to fear me if that is your concern. And please, watch your language young lady."

"I'm not afraid of anyone," she lied. In truth she was, at the very least, concerned by this man who had now entered her life twice and apparently knew who she was. "And I'll say whatever words I please."

"Of course, you are brave. But Graystone needs us."

"Graystone? How do you...wait, what's wrong, where is he," she asked as she pulled her phone from her hoodie again. Behind the pocket her stomach still burned dully. No new texts.

"Likely already on his way to the hospital. He was shot, or perhaps stabbed, but injured either way."

"How do you know that?"

"That is very difficult to explain at present," Robert said. "But I mean you no harm. I can take you to the hospital, but the sooner the better."

Kuin tried to call Graystone. Voicemail. She tried again. Voicemail again. She looked at the man. "Okay, but I want answers on the way."

Robert nodded. "I will do my best, though you may not understand them all. The most important..."

His words were cut off by Kuin fainting. He caught her easily and set her in his car. "Wake up child," he muttered under his breath, and her eyes fluttered open weakly.

"Okay," she mumbled.

He put his hand on her stomach, and the pain was gone. She felt stronger again, as if she hadn't just passed out. "What did you do," she asked.

"I eased things for you, for now. But we must hurry," he said as he closed her door and walked around the car.

"Are you some kind of witch or something?"

Robert laughed. "No, child, I am not a witch. Although I suppose the 'or something' could be fair."

She wanted to scoff at being called a child, but he punched the gas pedal and she shot back into her seat. She watched him in silence as he raced them toward the hospital.

****

Graystone's eyes opened, and the world was bright. Very bright, in fact, and he shielded his eyes from the sun. And it was warm. And there were mountains. Where was he? This was not Lorain, and it sure wasn't winter.

"Fight," a strong voice said.

"Fight who," Graystone asked.

"First, fight for your life," the voice answered. "Then you must fight alongside your sister against the master *u B'nakma*."

"Master of darkness? Who are you," Graystone asked, looking around. "Where are you?"

"Yes, the master of darkness. I am Gwimsum, and I am waiting for you and your sister to free me."

"I don't have a sister," Graystone said.

"You do, and you will see her soon. Find me. But for now, you must fight."

The last word was a yell so fierce that it reverberated through every bone in his body. There was a pain in his stomach again, that hot, burning pain. He squeezed his eyes shut, and when he opened them he saw lights passing above him. He was floating. No, not floating. He was rolling on a…cart? Gurney. He was on a gurney.

"Stay with me," a voice said, and he saw a doctor, or maybe a nurse. "We're going to take care of you, but you need to stay with me."

I need to fight, he thought. But then his eyes closed again, and the world went black.

✳✳✳

Kuin screamed out in pain again as Robert drove quickly towards the hospital.

"It is not your pain," he said.

"Who's is it?"

"You already know," he answered, not taking his eyes off of the road.

"What happened to him? What is happening to me?"

Kuin didn't realize that she had even asked the question out loud until the white haired man answered. "As I said earlier, he was shot or stabbed, I don't know which. When I touched you I could feel the wound, but it was too brief for me to tell what it was. And nothing is happening to you, not yet. It is happening to him."

✳✳✳

Graystone could feel himself open his eyes again, but he could see nothing. He could feel nothing. Was he dead? What in the actual hell was happening to him?

Dfif kpe 'B'nakma, a voice hissed from the dark.

In his mind Graystone pictured a snake talking to him. Was this the devil? He had never really believed in God, and God certainly had done nothing to help him.

"Welcome to the darkness," he repeated back to the voice, his tone a question.

You are where you belong, the voice said in its strange tongue. *I have waited for a body powerful enough to contain me. At long last, my wait is over. Open yourself, and I shall make you a king.*

Graystone spun in a circle in the complete blackness, flailing his arms in an effort to feel something. "Show yourself," he demanded.

You are looking at me, the voice hissed. *I am the darkness. Give yourself to me, that I may take form.*

"And why would I do that?"

Because I can make you the most powerful man in all of the worlds. You can leave the streets and your pathetic life behind. You can bring Kuin with you to a palace and a world beyond your imagination.

What the hell kind of dream was this? "I will fight. You are just my mind trying to convince me to give in to death."

You can fight, the voice hissed calmly. *And you will survive. Your body will live on in your world, Kuin visiting you for a while in the hospital before she tires of seeing your sleeping body. How long will she come to you? A few weeks? Months? Years maybe? How long until she decides that you will never awaken, and forgets you? Your mind will be here, trapped with me, trapped by me. I will let you hear her words when she visits you. Let you feel her touch as she holds your hand and begs you to wake up. I will laugh as you scream to her, and she will never know.*

"No, this isn't real. I will not give in to you."

The voice cackled. *You will, but will you do so before it is too late? Before the only friend, only family, that you have forgets you?*

3

When they arrived at Trinity hospital, Kuin and Robert ran into the emergency room. The woman at the desk wouldn't tell them anything at first, but when Robert insisted that he was the boy's uncle, she led them to another part of the hospital.

"The doctor will be with you as soon as he can," she said as she gestured them into a sitting area.

Robert thanked her and took a seat.

"I'm sure you have questions," he said, Kuin pacing back and forth across the small area. "Do you want me to get you anything," he asked when she didn't acknowledge him.

Kuin shook her head, but didn't speak. The pain was coming in waves in her stomach, and it was never as intense as that first time. A few times she even wondered if it was the phantom pain or just her own worry and concern clenching at her gut.

"Kuin, you must eat something. When was the last time you had anything to eat or drink?"

She stopped pacing and whirled on the man. "My best friend is possibly dying somewhere in this hospital, and you want me to eat? Do you think I care about eating or drinking right now?"

Robert sighed, a small but exasperated sigh. "Suit yourself. But if you do not take care of yourself, you will

not be able to help your friend. You need your strength.
He will be fine, I promise you that."

Kuin scoffed, but it didn't have the edge that she
had hoped for. It was softened by the tears that were
slowly rolling down her face. Kuin hated crying, and when
she cried it made her angry which only made her cry even
harder.

"You can't possibly know that," she said.

"I can, and I do. You must trust me. You are both
important, more important than you could possibly
imagine."

Kuin looked at the man for a moment. "Important to
whom? We are both street rats, discarded by society. We
steal to pay for a roof over our heads and food in our
stomachs. The only person that may care if we were never
seen again is Belly, and that is because we are profitable
to him. No one loves us, no one cares for us, and no one
would miss us."

Robert looked at her. The poor girl, he thought.
She had no idea the power in her, nor how valuable she
was to everyone, both in this world and his own. He finally
spoke. "You are important to me, and you are important to
a great many people, but you need to be strong. And to be
strong, you need to eat something, and rest. I'm going to
go get something for you, and then we will see to
Graystone."

Kuin just looked at him as he walked away.
Important to him? Important to 'a great many people'? He
didn't even know her, and the world certainly didn't care
about her. She sat down in one of the waiting room chairs.
It was not comfortable, but it was better than standing.

"Are you okay, dear," a kindly looking older lady
asked her. Kuin hadn't even noticed the woman before
now. She took the woman in, unsure how she managed to

miss her. She was usually very aware of everyone around her. Everyone was either a threat, or a mark. The woman had long black hair, and her eyes were so dark they nearly matched. Around her neck she wore a silver chain, with a large red gemstone. Ruby? All Kuin could think was how much she could get for it.

"My best friend has been shot, and I don't know what to do," she admitted before she could stop herself.

The woman stood from the seat that she was in, and came to sit beside Kuin. "Let the doctors care for him, he is in good hands. But you should be by him. Talk to him, tell him how much you need him. The power of encouragement cannot be understated. It may just help him to fight for his life."

"The doctors won't let us see him yet. They said that they will give us an update, but the waiting feels like it's taking forever."

Kuin nearly shuddered when the woman smiled. Her teeth were dark and rotten looking, and they all looked a bit sharp. "They will let you in soon, I'm sure. Just talk to him, be there for him. Hold his hand and tell him how much you need him. They say that it helps to hear the voice of a loved one."

The nurse came back and interrupted their conversation. "You can see him now, I'll take you."

Kuin stood and followed her down a hallway. "Is he okay?"

"The doctors can tell you more when you get to the room, but I can tell you he is stable. There is a chapel on the next floor up if you'd like to pray."

That seemed like a bit of an odd thing for the nurse to say. Then a thought hit Kuin. "Is it that bad? Is he going to die?"

The woman stopped, and turned to Kuin. "No, no, not at all. He's stable right now, I just thought that you might like somewhere private to pray."

Pray? I don't pray, Kuin thought. "Oh, no, I'm not religious."

"Oh, I'm sorry, I just heard you in the waiting room when I came in, and it sounded like you were praying."

Kuin was fully confused now. "What do you mean? I was talking to the other woman, she was encouraging me to stay by Graystone's side."

The nurse now had an expression of confusion that matched Kuin's own. "I didn't see another woman, I'm sorry. It sounded beautiful, whatever you were saying."

'Sounded beautiful'? What the hell was this lady talking about? "Thank you," was all Kuin said, confused and eager to see her friend.

****

When Robert returned to the waiting room with a sandwich and soda, Kuin was gone.

"Have you seen the girl I came in with," he asked the nurse at the desk.

The woman looked up and smiled. "Oh, yes, I just took her to your nephew's room. I can show you the way," she said as she stood from her chair.

As they walked to the room, the nurse turned to look at Robert. "Is she your niece?"

Robert nodded. "Yes, she is. She is Graystone's sister. Well, half sister, but they are as close as any siblings."

The nurse nodded. "I am a little worried that she may be in shock."

Robert's eyebrow raised. "Why do you say that?"

"Well, when I walked in to the waiting area it sounded like she was praying, but in another language. I thought maybe Latin, or some family prayer, sometimes folks come in whose parents or grandparents have taught them a prayer in the language of whatever country they came from. But she said that she wasn't praying." The nurse paused for just a beat. "But she said that she was talking to some woman in the waiting room with her. There was no one in there with her though. So, I don't know, I just thought maybe she was in shock. Does she have an active imagination?"

Robert nodded. "Yes, she does. I suppose she could be trying to comfort herself, but I'll be sure to keep an eye on her," he said with a reassuring smile.

The nurse smiled back, and continued leading him to the room.

Robert's smile was reassuring, but he was anything but comfortable. It couldn't be B'nakma already, he had no way of materializing. He needed a body, and Robert would have felt it had he taken one. Perhaps a demon, or one of his dreads, was here. He hadn't felt it, but he had been so preoccupied with the kids that he hadn't been focusing as he should. He was just about to reach out and feel for anything, or anyone, that didn't belong, when they arrived at the room.

"Here we are, the doctor will be in shortly," the nurse said before heading back to her desk.

Graystone lay in the hospital bed unconscious. Lead wires and IV's running from his body to various machines, beeping and whirring as they monitored his condition. Kuin held his hand and whispered in his ear, her eyes swollen, tears soaking her red cheeks.

Robert stood watching them, but only distractedly. He searched for any other presences from Hilcha. He felt no one, but if they had been speaking with Kuin in the waiting room, they would have left the moment the conversation ended. The effort to stay here physically, in this realm, was far too great. He would be more cautious, he assured himself. He would not let the girl out of his sight again.

****

Kuin's voice was as clear in his mind as the voice of the darkness. "I'm sorry I wasn't there."

Graystone tried to speak, willed his body to move, his mouth to utter the words in his head. But he knew by the way that Kuin did not so much as pause her speaking, she could not hear him. She went on and on about how strong he was, how he needed to fight, how much she needed him.

Would you leave her alone in the world? Would you let her mourn you while you yet live?

"I will not let you have me. None of this is real."

You're right, of course. It isn't real. I am only your subconscious. So, give in to me, free yourself from the prison of your mind, and hold her hand back. Hug her, speak to her, let her know everything will be okay.

It would be so easy to give in, Graystone thought. If he just let himself go to whatever it was that was pulling him, he could wake up. Wake up and move on. There would be peace and freedom.

Kuin continued to tearfully speak to him. *Go back and be with her. You wont even know the difference. Give in to me and you will be whole again.*

"No," Graystone screamed out.

Kuin's voice came into his mind again. "I don't know what is happening, but something's wrong. There is a man, and I've seen him before, he's the one that bumped into me and messed up my grab earlier. And then when you were shot, he suddenly was beside me, and he brought me here. I don't know who he is, and I don't know what to do. Please, I'm lost, and I need you. Fight, fight for me and wake up."

Go back to your friend. She needs you. Be there, don't make her do this life alone. When I make you a king, she can be there with you. She can sleep in a palace instead of a run-down theatre. She will never be hungry again. Do it for her.

And he wanted to. God knows he wanted to. He didn't believe in this dream he was having, but if all that he had to do was 'give in' to wake up and be with her again, maybe that would be for the best.

"Fine," he said to the darkness. "Fine, just let me wake up."

Yes. Good, wake up. But before I release your mind, you must give it over to me. Say the words I tell you to say, and you will wake up. Within days you will walk out of the hospital, and into a life you never could have imagined.

"I have imagined an awful lot of lives. I just want mine back."

Then repeat after me: wa oho fwim ho gbf.

"Wa oho fwim ho gbf," Graystone repeated, curious how he knew the words. 'You may have my mind'.

Wa oho fwim ho kmî.

"You may have my body," Graystone repeated in the strange language. Strange, yet not. It was somehow familiar. Like he had been speaking this language his whole life.

O wibta wa myîn the B'nakma ta dfeb ho byak.

"I free you from the darkness and into my light."

Graystone could feel Kuin's head on his shoulder. He could feel her tears warming his cheek and neck. He wrapped his free arm around her weakly.

Kuin shot up from his shoulder. "Graystone?"

By the time that she had sat up and looked into his green eyes, the black had left them and all that was left was his normal grey flecks.

"Hi," he said weakly.

4

It had been two days since Graystone had woken up, and the doctors were amazed by his progress.

"The wounds are healing faster than I have ever seen," the doctor had said that morning when he made his rounds. "I'd say he'll be ready to move within another day or so."

Kuin knew exactly what he meant by 'ready to move'. He had been shot by the police, the cop had only seen a young black man with something in his hand and pulled the trigger before taking time to see it was just a phone. But they had still posted an officer outside of the hospital door when Graystone regained consciousness. He was going to juvey for theft. And that was best case scenario. He was almost eighteen, so if the prosecutor decided he could charge Graystone as an adult.

"I'll be fine," Graystone said as if reading her mind.

The doctor excused himself.

"You're going to jail."

Graystone nodded. "Yeah, but I was shot and it's my first offense, so the prosecutor might go easy. Heck, I might even get off with just probation."

"Belly will never let you come back. You know the rules. If you're caught, you're out."

"Good. If I do go to jail, I'll come get you as soon as I'm out. And if I don't go to jail, then you can come with me straight away."

Before she could respond, Robert knocked gently on the door. "Actually, I've spoken to the prosecutor. I was able to convince him that I would take you in and make sure that you didn't get into any more trouble. No witness could identify you, and I convinced him that he didn't want a lawsuit, nor did he want Lorain to be put on the map for police brutality."

Kuin beamed, but Graystone was suspicious. "Why would you do that?"

Kuin had come to trust the man, which was highly unusual for her. But he had helped her get to the hospital, and he had stayed by her side, by both of their sides, the entire time.

"Because it was the right thing to do, and because I believe in second chances. You've been dealt a crap hand in life, you both have," Robert said, looking between the two, "and I believe you deserve better."

Graystone didn't buy it. "So out of the goodness of your heart, you've decided to help two kids? Are you just a bored rich guy that thought he might feel better if he helped out some poor street kids? Well, we're no charity case."

Kuin squeezed his hand. "Let's just focus on getting you better. For now, the best way to do that is to keep you out of jail and somewhere you can heal up. It sounds like Robert has done that."

"She's right. I understand you are suspicious, you've every right to be so. You have not been cared for in a very long time. Neither of you have, in fact," Robert said with a quick glance to Kuin. "But I assure you, I only want to help you."

Go with him, let him take you where you need to go.

This was the first time that Graystone had heard that voice since he had woken up. He jumped at the sound of it in his head.

"What's wrong," Kuin asked, "are you in pain? Do you need me to get the nurse?"

"No, no I'm fine." He was fine at the moment, physically at least. But he felt like he was going crazy. It had just been a dream, his brain convincing him to wake up when he was in his coma. Hadn't it?

Robert came over and took his hand. "Please, let's just focus on getting your better, and when you are all healed, if you want to leave you can. But I have a comfortable home with plenty of room, and good food in the fridge."

"Okay, but Kuin stays with me. I don't want her going back to Belly's."

"Of course, she is welcome as well. I would never separate the two of you."

"I'm going to go to the convenience store across the street. Do you want anything," Kuin asked.

Graystone shook his head.

"Would you join me, Robert?"

"Of course." He smiled and turned to Graystone. "We'll be right back, try to rest."

When Robert and Kuin left, Graystone closed his eyes. He would love to rest, he thought, but the voice had come back, and now when he closed his eyes he felt ill at the darkness.

I never left, I just had nothing to say.

"Jesus, you're real," Graystone exclaimed, his eyes shooting open.

Of course I'm real. Did you think that you were just lucky?

"I don't know, I guess. But you can't be real."

And yet here I am, talking to you. Watching you. Waiting.

"Waiting for what? No, no you are not real. You're just in my head. Trauma from being shot. That's all. I don't need you anymore, I just needed to wake up and my mind sent you to wake me up. But I don't need you, I'm awake."

Very well. I will leave you then.

"Just like that? "

Yig klinglik fuskem, the voice repeated. *Just like that.*

✳✳✳

"Why are you helping us," Kuin asked as they crossed the street. She trusted the man to some degree, but Graystone was right, Robert had no reason to be helping them.

When they reached the other side of the cross walk, Robert stopped and looked at Kuin. "Because I was friends with your parents."

Kuin felt like she had been slapped. "My parents? How?"

He took her hand in his. "I know that you don't remember them, the only life you know is the one on the streets. I know that you never have talked to Graystone about them, or your life before Belly, because you did things that you feel were wrong."

Tears pricked at her eyes, and she yanked her hand free. "You don't know anything."

"Your father's name is Fyan, and your mother's is Heekah. You feel things you can't explain, you know words that no one else does."

Kuin took a step back. Fyan? Heekah? "Why would you say that? I never knew my parents. Why would you say that? Are you trying to hurt me? Why?"

Robert stepped closer, and took her hand again. "No, child, sweet child. I would never try to hurt you. I said only what was true. I say it because you are my d'nu."

"How do you know that word," she asked, tear's freely streaming down her cheeks. She wanted to pull away, but she also felt a strange comfort in his hand. It almost felt like he actually was somehow her family, her d'nu.

"Because it is the native language of your parents. It is your native language."

"Not yours?" She didn't really know why she was even allowing this conversation to continue, why she didn't run away from this man that she was now suddenly remembering that she barely knew.

"No," he chuckled. "You wouldn't understand my native language. But I do speak Hilchan, and English."

"Hilchan?"

"Yes, that is what the people of Hilcha speak, your native tongue."

"I've never heard of it. What country is it in," she asked as she pulled her hand from his and grabbed her phone to search for 'Hilcha'.

"It is not in a country. It is not, in fact, of this world."

His words made her fingers stop typing on the phone. She knew that it sounded freaking crazy, but she also felt deep in her soul that he was telling the truth.

"Where is it," she asked quietly.

"Far from here. And we will go there as soon as Graystone is strong enough. But for now, I beg you to trust me. Please listen to me, and let me help you get home. I promise every question that you have will be answered then."

"Graystone will go with us?"

"Yes, it is his destiny as much as it is yours."

It seemed so crazy. So completely and utterly insane. But it also felt true. It felt like for the first time in her life, Kuin may actually have a home out there somewhere. Even if it was not on this world.

5

Kuin stayed by Graystone's side that night. She didn't know how Robert had convinced the hospital to allow her to stay past visiting hours, but she was grateful. The next morning, the three of them got into the Mercedes and left the hospital. Graystone sat looking out the window, eyes far away from the car.

"How far is your home," Kuin asked. She sat in the back seat with Graystone, making Robert almost look like a chauffeur.

"Not far. When we get there, I will show you both to the guest rooms, Graystone will be comfortable there while he continues to heal up."

"Thank you," Graystone said, barely a whisper.

"Of course. There are things that we need to discuss, however."

Kuin raised an eyebrow. "Like what?"

"Like getting the two of you out of Lorain, and to the place that I was telling you about." Robert glanced in the mirror and made eye contact with Kuin. "Sooner, rather than later."

"What place," Graystone said, turning his gaze to the driver for the first time.

Robert sighed. "I knew Kuin's parents. I am going to take her to the place where she was born, to her home."

With a wince, Graystone sat up straight and turned to Kuin. "What is he talking about? You already knew about this claim?"

"I did," she nodded. "And I believe him. I can't explain it, but I believe him. I know he's telling the truth."

"Kuin, this is crazy. You don't even know where your parents were from. All you know is that they died. And now, some old guy shows up and claims to have known them, and you agree to go with him to wherever it is that he wants to go?"

Robert coughed at being called an 'old guy', but other than that said nothing.

"I know, I know," Kuin said, resting her hand on his. "But I told you, I believe him. I don't know how to explain it. It's just a feeling."

"A feeling? You're letting him take us god knows where because of a feeling?"

Kuin just nodded.

"Fine. I'm not leaving your side. I don't like this, but I'm not leaving your side." Graystone said the words to Kuin, but was looking at the mirror and staring Robert in the eyes when he said it.

"Of course not," Robert said, looking away only to watch the road. "You are both welcome, and as I explained to Kuin, where we are going is just as much your home as it is hers."

"Where exactly are we going," Graystone asked, straightening in his seat. "And why would it be my home? I was born and raised here."

Robert told Graystone the same things that he had told Kuin, but Graystone stopped listening when he was told that Kuin wasn't from this world.

"Are you hearing this crap," he asked Kuin incredulously. "You can't actually be buying this? He's playing you, playing us."

"'He' is sitting right here," Robert cut in before Kuin could respond. "And I assure you, I'm telling you both the truth. If I were trying to scam you somehow, making up a story about other worlds certainly wouldn't be the most efficient way to gain your trust."

"I wasn't talking to you."

"I know it seems crazy, but I trust him. You know me, you know I'm not one to get played or scammed. I can't explain it, but I feel it. He's telling the truth. There is likely more to the story," Kuin said with a glance to Robert, "but he's not lying."

She's right, he's not lying. And you need to go with them to Hilcha.

Graystone grimaced at the sound of the darkness in his mind. He didn't like having the voice in his mind, and he didn't trust Robert. But Kuin did.

"Fine, but I want answers. And I want them tonight. Food, a shower, probably more food, and then I want answers."

"We'll talk when you've gotten settled," was all Robert said as they drove in silence the rest of the drive.

Robert's home did not disappoint. It was a home that had always been one of Kuin's favorites to dream about when she would go past it. It was old and regal looking, on the edge of Lorain, four large columns held up a porch above the front door, and the house itself was gated. Robert put in a code, and the gate slid silently back, lights flicking to life along the driveway.

"Fancy," Graystone said, a bit excited to stay somewhere this nice, and a bit annoyed at it's pretentiousness.

"It's comfortable, and you will have a quiet place to gain your strength back."

As they pulled near, and drove into the garage, the size of the house came clearly into view. From the front it looked comfortable, but up close it was clear that it was a mansion.

"It's huge," Kuin said, with wonder in her eye and a smile on her face at the prospect of not being cramped into an attic room.

"It last belonged to one of the basketball guys in Cleveland, but when he got traded last year, I was able to get a good deal on it. He left all of the furnishings, so I didn't have to do much."

When Robert opened the door, classical music began playing softly from the built-in speakers.

Graystone glanced at Kuin who simply smiled. "Bolero?"

Robert smiled back at her. "You enjoy classical?"

"Some. I've always liked this one. It begins so soft, but it ends in such a flourish of sound."

Graystone just sighed and muttered something under his breath that sounded an awful lot like 'siddity' to Robert. "Shall I show you to your rooms?"

Robert didn't wait for a reply and began walking toward the staircase in the center of the home. It curved gracefully to a lavish balcony. "This way," he said when they reached the top.

Stopping in front of a set of double doors, Robert held out a hand in the direction of the room. "This is the first guest suite, and the next set of doors is the second. They are both essentially the same size and have their own bathrooms. If you would be more comfortable sharing a room, I could-"

"Yes," Graystone said, at the exact same time as Kuin said "no".

Robert cleared his throat. "Yes, well, if you'd like I have an air mattress that I could set up, or you can both have your own space. I will leave that to you. I'm going to go down and prepare some food while you two get comfortable."

He began walking away, but stopped at the top of the stairs. "I know that you do not trust me, Graystone. And I know that you have no reason to. I would like you to know, however, that I am incredibly glad to have found you and your," he hesitated just a moment, so short Kuin wasn't sure that he even had, "friend. You both are more important than you could imagine, and I have hoped for this moment for many years. Rest up, come down when you are ready."

As he turned and silently descended the stairs, Kuin could've sworn that his eyes glistened.

6

"I'm just saying that I'd be more comfortable if you were in here with me, we don't know him."

Kuin rolled her eyes as she sat down in the armchair across from Graystone's bed. "I'm not worried about him, I'm literally in the room right next to you, and I am not giving up my chance to have a whole bedroom and bathroom to myself for the first time in my life."

"Fine," he said with a sigh. "But, I'm going to be keeping an eye out."

Kuin stood and kissed her friend on the forehead. "Whatever makes you happy. I'm going to take a hot shower, and then eat some of whatever our host has for dinner."

In her own room, Kuin closed the door. She thought about diving onto the bed but decided she would rather take a shower first. She felt filthy from the hospital and the lack of clothes to change into while she was there. Crap. She still didn't have any clothes to change into. Her phone vibrated. It was a picture from Graystone. She opened it, the caption reading '**kinda creepy that he knew my size?**' under a picture of what looked like the dresser in his room, full of clothes.

Kuin walked to her own dresser and let out a small squeal when she saw that it was fully stocked with clothes, and she giggled just a little when she opened the walk-in closet to find it full of everything from jeans to dresses in her size.

no not weird. he's been with you at the hospital for a couple days, could've seen your size or guessed close enough. jumping in shower.

With that she tossed her phone on the bed and went into the bathroom. The shower was like something out of a movie. There were jets and shower heads on every wall, and a clear glass door that had a control panel next to it. Kuin selected 'relax' from the preset options, and the shower came to life. She climbed in and for the next fifteen minutes (or maybe longer, it was really relaxing) she let herself think of nothing but the shower.

When she had finished her shower and dressed in some very comfortable sweatpants and an oversized tee shirt that she found in the closet, Kuin made her way back downstairs. She had stopped at Graystone's door, but he hadn't answered when she knocked.

As soon as she reached the bottom of the staircase, the smell of tomatoes, garlic, and pasta made her stomach growl. "That smells amazing," she said as she entered the kitchen.

Modern and large, with a spacious island in the middle, Robert moved effortlessly around it as he mixed, and stirred, and adjusted the heat on the stove.

"Ah, well, I am a competent cook, but I must admit, most of it is just store bought. The bread, however," he said as he opened the oven and pulled out a pan with what looked to be an amazing garlic knot loaf, "I did make from scratch."

"I can tell you that it will all be much appreciated, and after days of hospital food, I cannot wait to eat something real."

"And eat you shall," he said as he set three spots at the table.

"When do we have to leave?"

Robert seemed surprised by the sudden question from Kuin, but answered it quickly as he continued to move food to the table. "As soon as we can. I would love to leave tomorrow, but I fear your friend may need or want to rest up for a day or two more."

"He seems to be doing okay, but I don't think he trusts you or the story you tell."

"I don't blame him," Robert said with a sigh, "he hasn't had many people in his life that he can trust, and I certainly have thrust quite a bit upon the two of you. He isn't wrong to be skeptical, and I must ask, why do you trust me?"

Kuin just shrugged as she pulled one of the still steaming garlic knots from the loaf. "If you wanted to hurt me, you could have done it at any time. You could have done it the night you brought me to the hospital, when I was feeling Graystone's pain. And the fact that I was feeling that pain, lends some credibility to the idea that something more than the ordinary is going on. I don't really have anything to keep me here, and since you don't appear to be a threat, I may as well see where this all goes."

Robert sat down at the table. "Fair enough. You said in the car that you thought I wasn't telling you the whole story."

Kuin just nodded as she began making her plate.

"You are correct. There is more to it. You are not just from Hilcha, you are special. Your parents were special. And there is danger there for you. But I will protect you with my life, and there are many in Hilcha that would do the same. I promise that I will explain every detail when we get there. There are things that will be much easier to show you than to tell you. Things that you may not believe if I just tell you."

"Like what," Graystone cut in from the doorway.

"Ah, you're awake. Please, have a seat. Eat."

Graystone sat across from Kuin. "What wouldn't we believe?"

"Most anything that I tell you, it would seem. But there is more to the story of the two of you. The fact that you found each other, formed a strong bond, and stood by each other is not surprising but it is fortunate. It saves time having to find the two of you separately."

"That doesn't answer my question. In fact, it just raises more," Graystone said as he spooned some pasta and sauce onto his plate.

"Indeed. Which is why I will not attempt to explain to you now. It will be much easier to show you. Explaining before you have seen Hilcha will simply raise more questions. I could spend days, weeks even, explaining everything to you and you still wouldn't understand. Not truly."

"How are you feeling? Do you think you will be okay to travel tomorrow," Kuin interjected.

Graystone just shrugged.

"If you feel up to it, it is about a ten-hour drive from here to Salem. Once there, it will only take a few minutes and we will be able to go to Hilcha."

"Salem? Like the witches," Graystone asked with a raised eyebrow.

Robert nodded. "Yes. The magic there is strong, and I do not have the power I once did to get to Hilcha without assistance."

"Magic," Graystone scoffed.

"Yes, magic. The thing that allowed Kuin to feel when you had been hurt. The thing that connects the two of you together in ways that you may have never really thought about but aren't quite normal. The thing that allowed me to come here, to find you, and the thing that will bring you home again."

Graystone shook his head and looked at Kuin. "Are you buying this?"

"I don't know," she said honestly. "But it would explain some things, and what do we have to lose?"

Graystone lowered his eyes and poked at his pasta with his fork. "I don't know, our lives?"

Robert chuckled. "If you mean at my hands, no. If I wanted to do you harm, I would have done so days ago. But you're not wrong. There are dangers in Hilcha, just as there are dangers here. There are those that would see harm come to the two of you."

"Why? Why would we go somewhere that has people that want to harm us? Why shouldn't we stay here, where we are safe?"

"I cannot make you go. But if you want a reason, I will say because it is your home. Because the magic she has in her will only truly be awakened there. And because she," Robert pointed his fork at Kuin, "is the Princess of Hilcha, and the heir to the throne."

Kuin choked on the pasta she was swallowing. "Princess?"

"Princess. And heir to the throne," Robert repeated. "Yes, there are dangers in Hilcha that you will not face here on earth. But there is also an entire people who are relying on you to come home, and an entire army that will protect you with their final breath if need be. It is my hope that it will not come to that though."

"You never said that I was the princess. That makes my father, what, the king?"

Robert shook his head. "No, it's not a patriarchy. The women hold the power in Hilcha. Your father is a very strong warrior, and a wise advisor, but it is your mother that rules. Or, at least, that's how it was."

"What do you mean, was," Graystone asked.

"I've been here, on earth, searching for you since you were taken more than fourteen years ago," he said looking to Kuin. "I haven't returned to Hilcha, nor would I have ever done so had I not found you. So, I do not know the situation there. It is possible that your mother no longer rules. It is possible that they have moved on to some other place, left royalty all together. I don't know."

"So when we go back, they may not even be waiting?"

The sadness in Kuin's face when she asked this nearly broke Robert.

"No," he shook his head, "there is no doubt that they will be waiting. They would never give up on you. The truth is, they do not know that I am here. They may very well think me lost the same as you. But I do know, beyond any doubt, that their love for you would never let them give up on seeing you again. When we return, they will be besides themselves to see you, I can assure you of that."

Graystone started to ask a question, but as he began to speak his eyes went black. Before Robert could do anything, Kuin stood and her monotone voice rang out, as if amplified.

"The spies are everywhere, the children they will find. Only by returning and bringing Gwimsum's light to the world again will B'nakma be defeated for a final time. A decision must be made, the fate of one, or the future of all."

As soon as she spoke the last word, Kuin and Graystone both crumpled to the floor.

7

Kuin awoke in her bed, Robert standing over her with his eyes closed and mumbling something under his breath.

"What happened? Where is Graystone?"

Robert's eyes shot open. "Graystone is in his bed, he woke before you and is resting. As for what happened, I do not know. There is much that I don't understand, but I believe that you gave us a prophecy."

"A prophecy," Kuin asked as she sat up. "I don't remember anything."

Robert repeated back what she had said and told her of what had happened. "I am not as knowledgeable on these things as your parents are, which is yet another reason why we must return as soon as we can. I wish to leave at first light. Rest tonight, and we will begin our journey tomorrow."

Kuin simply nodded and watched as Robert turned and left her room. She would rest, she thought, but not until she checked on Graystone.

She entered her friend's room silently. He appeared to be sleeping peacefully, and when she touched his hand he didn't stir. She sat down beside his bed and spoke softly to him.

"I'm sorry that I dragged you into this. You have been the best friend that I could ever hope for, and you deserve better than this. I know you don't believe what he's told us, but I do. More now than ever. I'm going to go to Hilcha, and I'm going to figure out what is happening. But you don't have to go, you'll be eighteen soon. You can do anything you want, start a real life."

She squeezed his hand gently, not wanting to wake him. "We'll talk in the morning. Just know I'm sorry," she said, resting her head on his shoulder.

He could hear her speaking, but he could not speak. He couldn't even move.

You must go to Hilcha with her, B'nakma's voice hissed in his mind. *Once we are there, I will fulfill my promise and make you a king.*

"This isn't real," Graystone answered. "None of this is real. There are no other worlds, there is no magic."

B'nakma chuckled in the boy's mind. *You know that's not true. You may have believed that when you made the deal with me, but you know better now. And the deal is set. So go to Hilcha with your friend. Soon I will be free, and this will all be over.*

"Free of what," Graystone asked, but B'nakma was gone.

✱✱✱

The next morning, after a quick but mostly silent breakfast, the three of them got into Robert's car.

"I need to stop for gas, and then we will be on the road until we need fuel again. If you want to grab snacks, please do so when we stop."

After he pumped the gas, Robert and Kuin went in to grab some snacks. Graystone stayed in the car, having barely spoken all morning.

"Is he okay," Robert asked when they were inside.

Kuin shrugged. "I don't know. This is all hard on him, and I think the only reason he is even here is for me. If I thought I could convince him to stay here, I would. But he is stubborn, and he loves me, so he will go anywhere I go."

Robert nodded. "He is your d'nu. And he is just as important as you are. You may be the princess, but he has a part to play in saving Hilcha as well. We will need both of you if we are to survive what is coming."

Kuin stopped and looked at him. "What actually is coming? And how is he a part of this? I'm from Hilcha, but he's not." Kuin paused and then raised an eyebrow. "Or is he?"

"Darkness is coming, a darkness that only the two of you with your people at your back can defeat. And to answer your question, yes, he is from Hilcha. He doesn't have the same power and magic that you do, but he is instrumental in all of this just the same."

Every time that they talked about her home, she seemed to end up with more questions than answers. "Why wouldn't you have told us that before?"

Robert smiled and began shopping again. "Would you have believed me? Or even if you did, would he have believed me?"

Kuin knew that he was right, Graystone doubted everything that Robert said, and he certainly wouldn't have accepted that he too was from another world. She was about to say as much when she saw a woman standing next to the car. "Who is that," she asked, pointing outside.

"Who is what," Robert asked, confused.

"The woman next to the car. What is she doing?"

It seemed as if she was bent down, speaking through the window to Graystone.

"I don't see anyone," Robert replied, more confused than before.

Kuin ran outside. Robert put down the snacks that they had grabbed, and ran after her. "Kuin, wait!".

As soon as she got outside, she saw that it was the same woman that had spoken to her in the hospital while Graystone was still unconscious.

"You! What are you doing," she yelled at the woman as she got closer.

"Gbub dnil," the woman yelled back.

Kuin didn't register that the woman had spoken in Hilchan. *Not yet,* she had said.

Without thinking, she answered in the same tongue. "Not yet? Who are you?"

The woman smiled a wicked smile, and when she did her façade of a kindly old woman fell away. She was still old, ancient even. Her pale skin was wrinkled and sagging. Her smile showed a mouth full of sharp, pointed teeth. But it was her eyes that truly shocked Kuin. Eyes of pure black. "Not yet," the crone repeated. "And I, dear princess, am the hand of B'nakma."

When Kuin ran towards her, the woman held up a hand and Kuin lifted into the air. Unable to move, she floated a few feet above the ground. "Not yet. We will meet again. I will be at full power, and you will die. You and anyone who stands with you will be swallowed by B'nakma. His rebirth will mark your demise."

Kuin found herself unable to move or speak.

"Kyil kpi bnegb ta iw," Kuin heard Robert say. *Reveal yourself and release her.*

The woman's smile disappeared, and Kuin dropped to the ground. With what looked like a puff of oily black smoke, she was gone.

Robert scooped up Kuin, put her in the car, and sped off.

"What the hell was that," she practically screamed.

"That was Yaswi," Robert said, shaking his head. "I couldn't see her until I commanded her to reveal herself. She is your great aunt. Or at least partly. B'nakma seduced her with empty promises, and her jealousy and ambition led to her betraying your family. She offered herself to B'nakma willingly, and allowed one of his demons to inhabit her body. Yaswi may still be in there somewhere, but more than likely it is only the demon. We thought her gone, dead or banished with B'nakma. Clearly she is not."

"I saw her before, at the hospital. When I was in the waiting room when Graystone…oh god, Graystone," Kuin said whirling to look at her friend. They had left so quickly that she had not even checked to make sure he was okay.

Graystone did not say anything. His eyes were closed, but Kuin could see his chest rising and falling. "Graystone," she called out, turning to the back seat and shaking him.

"She trapped him. We must get to Hilcha now, we cannot go to Salem," Robert said without taking his eyes off of the road.

"How? I thought we had to use the magic in Salem? And trapped him where?"

"Where he is, I'm not sure. But getting him to Hilcha will be the best, and likely only, way to free him. As for Salem, it would be easier to travel from there. I have been here for a long time, and I have used much magic to find you. Less would be needed in Salem. But we no longer have the time to wait. We must go to the Myeb. It is our way now."

"The Myeb? As in the rundown restaurant? Is it even open?"

"No, it is not," Robert nodded, "But it is our closest way to Hilcha. Unfortunately, because of its age it also has the weakest magic, making it more difficult. But I can do it."

8

As they raced up Route Six, Lake Erie off to the right, Kuin continued to try to wake up Graystone. She had crawled between the front seats and into the back next to him.

"Open his eyes, and tell me what you see."

Kuin did as Robert had said and let out a sharp gasp. "They…they're black," she stammered.

Robert cursed under his breath. "Take his hand."

When Kuin had, Robert reached back and grabbed her free hand. "Reveal to us the place in which his mind resides," he said in Hilchan.

Suddenly, the world went dark and Kuin could see nothing. She could feel the car begin to slow, she could feel the two men's hand's in hers, she could hear the sound of the road and Robert saying something, but she could see nothing.

Robert's words finally became clear. It was as if he had gone from a far-off muffled voice, to screaming directly into her head. "Let go of our hands!"

Kuin released his hand, and she felt the car jerk violently one way, and then the other. But she could not remove her hand from Graystone's. Despite trying to jerk it away, she felt as though she couldn't move at all.

Hello princess, a voice, low and slithering, hissed in her mind. Her mind tried desperately to escape, but her body would not move.

I cannot hold you here for long. It is too much to hold you both, my powers are not yet full. When I have physical form, I will see you again.

"B'nakma," Kuin said the name, knowing to whom the voice must belong.

Yes, and soon you will see me. Soon you will meet me face to face, though I suspect you will wish that you had not. But our paths will meet, nothing can stop that. When they do, I shall end you and your entire family line, and in doing so I will free myself from the prison I am confined to. But, before I let you go, a smile crept into his voice, *allow me to leave you with a gift.*

Pain unlike anything Kuin had ever felt coursed through her entire body. She tried to scream, but found herself unable to do anything.

Now you know what your friend will suffer until I am free. Every moment between now and then, he will burn with my darkness. And when I am free, I shall entrap every person of your bloodline in a prison of endless pain. Goodbye for now, I'll see you soon.

Suddenly she was screaming in the backseat of the car, her hand no longer holding Graystone's.

"What did you see," Robert asked, not slowing.

"Nothing, I saw absolutely nothing."

"B'nakma," Robert said, a bit shakily. "Did he say anything to you?"

She recounted what had happened while she was in the darkness, and Robert swore. "We are almost there."

Kuin looked around. "I can't believe Myeb is a way to another world."

"Yes. The magic of this area is strong, or at least was. As it began to fade, those that knew of it's power built the Myeb out of Amherst Sandstone. The magic of the land ran strong through the stone, and the Myeb was a portal to other worlds for many years. But as things changed, those that were caretakers of the magic stopped maintaining it. The natural, raw magic is all that remains. It is not as strong as in Salem, but we no longer have time to travel. There are things that you need to know, however."

"No crap," Kuin said. The pain from the darkness still echoed in her mind. Her friend was trapped there. The building that she had walked past hundreds of times in her life held magic to take her to a different world, her world. There was plenty that she still needed to know.

"I do not know how much I will be drained by taking us through the portal. I am not who you think I am. On the other side, you may not recognize me. I may revert to my true form."

"True form," Kuin raised an eyebrow.

"Yes, but there is no time to explain, and it may be that I do not change," Robert said flatly as the bridge approached.

The pothole filled parking lot of Myeb did not impress. As soon as the car stopped, Robert grabbed Graystone from the backseat. Kuin thought briefly of how many times she had snuck behind this very building, imagining that the castle was real and not a run-down restaurant The irony that the building actually did hold magic was not lost on her. She may have been able to go home years ago if she had only known.

As they approached the building, Kuin could feel the air changing. It almost felt as if it was electric. Her hair began to fluff up, and her skin tingle. By the time they reached the door, the air smelled metallic, and she could taste the tang of it in her mouth.

When they entered, Robert turned to face Kuin. In his hand tucked between himself and Graystone was a necklace with a beautiful diamond set in silver. The stone seemed to roil on the inside, like smoke wafting through the air. "Wear this. If something happens to me, or we get separated, show this to whomever you see first. They will help you."

When she put it around her neck and tucked it under her shirt, Robert swiftly turned back around and led her down a set of stairs and into the basement of the restaurant. They reached a solid stone wall with what looked like a doorway carved into it. Robert called out in a strong, commanding voice. "Dfik kwa kpan u Hilcha. Fipupkum chow yan kpe a potyip."

Open for the children of Hilcha. Let them return to their rightful home.

The stone that made up the doorway crumbled away to nothing, and a bright blue light pulsed inside, and a loud buzz filled the air.

"Go," Robert urged Kuin.

"Together," she demanded, pointing at Graystone. "I need to know that he is with me."

Robert looked at the motionless form in his arms. "Take my hand then," he said above the sound of the portal.

With Robert holding Graystone, and Kuin holding Robert's hand, they crossed into the bright light. The stone resealed, and then they were gone.

The man had been walking home from the market, humming as he carried the sack of fresh vegetables for dinner, when he saw the young girl stumbling along the path. She looked like she could barely stand up, and he rushed to her.

"Are you okay," he asked when he got to her. He set his sack down and grabbed her just as she was about to fall.

"I think so," Kuin said. "Where am I?"

She wore strange trousers, and a hooded cloak that he thought was too big for her small frame. She had a small cut on her temple that was trickling blood down her cheek.

"Sit," he said, lowering her into the grass next to the road. "You're in Dwer. What's your name, child?"

Kuin shook her head. "I…I don't know," she answered.

"That's okay," the man said as he wiped her forehead with his sleeve. "You look like you hit your head. Are you alone?"

"I don't know," Kuin said again, this time panic starting to creep into her voice.

"Okay, okay. I live only a couple of more minutes down the road, I was just returning from the market. My wife can help you clean your wound, and we can get you some fresh water and some food. Can you walk?"

"I think so," Kuin said as she stood slowly.

"I'll help you, come."

As they walked, a cat came running up behind them, and rubbed against Kuin's leg. "Is he yours?"

Kuin looked at the cat. He was beautiful. His fur was all white, his right eye a bright blue, while his left eye was a golden yellow. There was something about his eyes that tickled her memory, but it was like a picture just out of focus. Her voice cracked as she again said that she didn't know.

        "Okay, no problem. He seems to like you. He
reminds me of a cat that I once had. He can come along,
maybe he will help you remember something."
        They walked the next couple of minutes in silence,
Kuin holding on to the man's arm for support. They
approached a lovely farmhouse with a wraparound porch.
        "Arpi, come quick, and bring water," the man called
out when they entered the home.
        As he sat Kuin down in a chair, she noticed for the
first time what he looked like. He was maybe fifty years
old, and his head was shaved. The beard he wore came
halfway down his chest.
        "What's wrong," a woman's voice came as she
entered the room.
        "She was wandering the road. I think she hit her
head."
        "Oh dear," the woman said, setting down a tray
with a glass and a pitcher of water on a table in the middle
of the room. "Let me see that cut."
        The cat that had followed them rubbed up against
the woman's leg. She was maybe ten years younger than
the man, and absolutely stunning. When she saw the cat,
she smiled and her dimples shone. "Hello boy," she said
rubbing the cat's head once.
        "He followed us home. I think maybe he belongs to
her, but she can't remember anything."
        The woman took a small towel from the tray and
dipped it in the water, gently cleaning Kuin's cut.
        "Well we'll get you cleaned up, and then we'll see if
we can't figure out who you are."
        After she cleaned the cut, the man handed Kuin a
glass of the water. "Drink up. We have dinner cooking
too, so you can have some food. I'm sure we can find you

something to wear, though it will likely be too big, but it will be clean at least."

"Does anything else hurt dear," the woman asked, gently running her hand over Kuin's shoulder.

"No, I think I'm okay," Kuin said.

The woman nodded. "Very well. I'll show you to the washroom and get you some clean clothes. I will also send word to see if anyone in town knows who you are."

Kuin's face fell at the reminder that she had no idea who she was, nor where she was.

"Don't worry, I'm sure it's just the bump on your head. Rest up and we will find your people."

Leaving Kuin to wash up, the woman returned to her husband. "She's scared. You just found her on the path?"

"Yes," he nodded, "she looked like she could barely stand. She wasn't coming from town, she was coming towards it. Perhaps she is from one of the mountain clans in the north, maybe from Paf."

The woman shrugged. "Perhaps. But if she is from Paf, that would be one hell of a journey for a child to be making alone. And did you see her clothes? I've never seen anything like those in any of our lands."

The man walked over to his wife and rubbed her shoulders. "Well, she stumbled into the right place. We will help her find her family, and we will care for her until she does."

The woman's body relaxed, the tension slipping out of her. "Yes, we will. She would be about that age if..."

"I know," her husband answered. "I thought the same thing."

The cat came in and rubbed against their legs.

"And what about you? I bet you know exactly who she is, don't you handsome boy," the man asked as he crouched down and rubbed the cat's head.

The cat meowed quite loudly and stared directly at the man.

"I think he's trying to tell you," the woman said with a smile.

9

Graystone opened his eyes. He was in a bedroom; he knew that much. Sitting up in the bed his eyes began to adjust. The walls were made of some sort of black stone, and the floor a dark wood. The windows had no dressings, and he could see the moon. He walked to the window and could see that he was in a tower, at least four or five stories up. No, that can't be right, he thought. He could see two moons. The light from them was casting an odd orange hue throughout the room. The air was hot and heavy, and it smelled acrid.

"Where am I," he mumbled as he went to the door.

Potyip, B'nakma's voice answered in his head. Home.

"Home? I think the hell not," Graystone said back as he opened the door. "Where is Kuin? What have-"

His words were cut off when he saw the creature outside his door. At least seven feet tall, and black as night it looked at him. It's body was muscular, but it's face was gaunt, hollow. Where there should have been eyes, there was only empty holes with smoke wisping in them. The thing smiled at him.

"Yes boy, home," it snarled through its razor-sharp teeth.

It seemed to enjoy Graystone's discomfort, and at his shiver, the thing unfurled large, sinewy wings.

"Jesus Christ," Graystone practically squealed, and retreated into the bedroom, slamming the door.

As he walked backwards, the creature came through the door. It didn't open the door, it just walked through it, as if it wasn't there.

"What are you?"

The toothy grin returned. "I am B'nakma. Do you see why I needed your body? This form is," he flexed his muscles and flapped his wings, "powerful, but it is not yet fully physical. I need your body to take on a full physical form."

"You aren't real," Graystone said, shaking his head wildly back and forth, "none of this is real."

"Of course it is, boy," B'nakma hissed. "And we have a deal. Don't worry. I was going to kill you, but now I think it will be more fun to leave you alive inside. Cut off from the world, so you can watch as I conquer it. You can watch as I kill your precious Kuin."

Graystone continued backing up from B'nakma, and soon was up against a window opening.

"No, you cannot have my body," he said.

As he silently begged Kuin to forgive him, he threw himself out of the window. The ground below came rushing at him.

"Nice try, but pointless," he heard B'nakma say, a smile in his voice.

The ground was so close that he thought he could touch it. He closed his eyes, prepared to hit the hard stone below. Instead, talons dug into his shoulders, and powerful wings flapped. B'nakma flew him back up the tower that he had just jumped from. Dropping him on the very top.

"Now then, about my body," B'nakma said through bared teeth. He lunged at Graystone, and all the boy

could think was how much he wished the ground had
gotten him instead.

Kuin sat straight up in bed and realized that she
was screaming. The couple that had helped her, Arpi and
her husband Klop, came rushing in. The woman lit a small
candle next to Kuin's bed. They had been kind enough to
allow her to sleep there for the night.

"What's wrong, child," Arpi said, sitting beside her
on the bed.

"I don't…nothing…it was just a dream I guess,"
Kuin stammered.

The woman rubbed her hair. "Tell us, and we can
banish it."

Banish a dream? That seemed a bit odd to Kuin,
but why not? She told them about the boy, and the
strange demon that had taken over his body. The boy felt
familiar, but she had no way of knowing why given that she
still couldn't remember her own name. As she told the
story, the faces of the other two in the room darkened.

"That may not have been a dream," Klop said.

"If not, and B'nakma has found a host…", the
woman trailed off, her gaze at the floor.

"If he has then it is a problem for your niece," the
man said.

The woman's gaze snapped to him. "Briyul is not
equipped to handle this."

"And you are not the queen anymore, Heekah," her
husband answered quietly.

Something in Kuin stirred. "Heekah? I thought
your name was 'Arpi'."

The woman chuckled softly. "No, sweet child, my name is Heekah, and my dear husband is Fyan. Arpi and Klop are simply pet names, terms of endearment if you will, that we have used for years."

Fyan? Heekah? Why did these names seem familiar. It was like a splinter in the back of her head, poking at her, trying to break through. The cat must have followed the adults into her room and howled loudly. Kuin groaned and slapped the bed in frustration.

Heekah put her hand on Kuin's shoulder. "I'm sorry child, we never meant to deceive you. I suppose we just didn't think about it."

Kuin shook her head. "It's not that. The boy, in my dream. I know him from somewhere. And your names, Heekah and Fyan," she said looking between the couple, "I know those names. I just don't know how I know them, and I can't connect it."

The woman brushed the hair out of Kuin's face, tucking it behind her ears. She rested her hands on Kuin's shoulders. "We will figure it out. Rest for now, and when the morning comes and light returns, we can take you into the village. Perhaps someone will know who you are, or who your relations are."

Kuin reached out and hugged Heekah. She held her for just a moment, and then thanked her. As the two adults left the room, Kuin could've sworn she saw the slightest glimmer of tears in the woman's eyes.

The next morning, Kuin woke to the smell of food wafting into her room. Her stomach growled fiercely at her, and she hurried up and put on the clothes that her host's had given her the night before.

"That smells amazing," Kuin said, and staggered. Another memory, there at the edges of her mind. A man with white hair cooking pasta. She had felt safe with him, but the boy didn't trust him. Gray…Grayson? That didn't feel right, but the name wouldn't reveal itself to her.

Fyan reached out and steadied her. "Are you okay?"

Kuin nodded as he helped her to a chair. "Yes. Just another memory. A man, with white hair, cooking pasta. And the boy from my dream, I almost had his name. It was right there. I almost called him Grayson, but that isn't it, I know it's not."

Fyan slid her a cup of something light purple and fruity smelling. "Drink some juice, eat a little food, and we'll try to figure it out. You said it was an old man cooking," he asked.

Kuin was delighted by the soft flavor of the drink, despite it being unlike any fruit she had ever tasted. "No," she shook her head. "He wasn't old. He just had white hair. And my friend, the boy from my dream, at least I think he was my friend, he didn't trust the man. Robert," she said excitedly.

The cat howled and ran over from the corner of the room, leaping onto the table. "Not where we eat," Fyan said gently pushing the cat off. "What on Hilcha is a 'Robert'," he asked.

Kuin shook her head. "No, Robert was his name. He was a friend too, I think. Damn it," she yelled in frustration. "I can't remember!"

Heekah entered the room. "It's okay, we'll help you remember, and we'll be here for you until you do," she said gently rubbing Kuin's back.

Kuin stood and went to the other side of the table. "No, no I need to do this now. The man's name was

Robert. He had white hair. Robert, Robert," she paused for a moment in thought. "Steekus! His last name was Steekus," she smiled with a sense of small victory.

Heekah gasped. Fyan put his hand on his wife's shoulder. "Robert Steekus? Bo Steekin," he said, a question in his voice.

The cat came and jumped back up onto the table. He turned in circles, over and over. Fyan reached out and rubbed his head and the cat closed his eyes. "The boy, the boy from your dream. Not Grayson," he said, tears in his eyes.

Heekah sobbed for a moment, and then looked at her husband. "Graystone."

The cat howled and ran over to Kuin. He stretched up from the table and pawed furiously at her neckline, at the necklace under her shirt. She reached in and removed it.

The sound's that came from Heekah and Fyan were guttural. Grief, loss, happiness, love. All of the emotions that a person could have were released with those sounds. "Kuin," Heekah managed to say.

"My sunshine," her father choked out between sobs.

When she heard her name, it all came back to her. "Den," she said, looking at the woman as if truly seeing her for the first time. *Mother.* "Yom," she said, reaching her arms out. *Father.*

As the three embraced, the cat, Bo, curled onto the floor between their feet, and purred contentedly.

10

She has returned, an ethereal voice purred.

The priest sitting alone in his modest hut knew of whom the voice spoke. The girl had not been lost but had been taken. He had felt the return of B'nakma, felt as his physical form strengthened. "But she was gone for so long. She doesn't remember who she truly is. She has been told, but all that she remembers is her time in the other world."

You will help her to remember. Train her, free her from the chains of her captors.

The priest sighed and opened his eyes. Standing from the pillow he sat on, he walked to the window of his modest hut. He lived alone on the island. The island was so small, there was really only room for one small dwelling. One priest at a time lived here. A priest had to commit to ten years on the island, but at the end of his commitment he could stay as long as he wished to serve. Glem was nearing his fifty-eighth year, and had served alone on the island for forty-two of those summers.

"I don't like children," he said, looking out across the water to the mountains rising in the south.

The voice chuckled. *You are but a child yourself. The oldest of us is ten times your age.*

It had taken Glem nearly to the end of his first decade on the island to hear the voice of one of the Mothers. His faith had faltered, and he prepared to leave after his commitment. He had nearly left early, in fact. He had missed his parents, his brothers and sisters, and the girl that he had wanted to court. He had missed his home. After seven silent years, he had drank more than he should have of his wine, and had packed his few belongings onto a boat and prepared to leave. But he had stayed instead.

"I know," he answered. "I will do as you ask. But if I am to train the girl, who will take my spot here?"

We will take care of that. Come to the Isle.

Glem was too stunned to respond immediately. Men were not allowed on the Isle of the Mothers, except for when invited, and then only were they allowed to enter the temple at the very edge of the island. No man had stepped foot on that sand for hundreds of years. So long had it been in fact, that the actual record of who the last man to enter the temple was, was lost to time. "I…I am to come…to you," Glem stammered.

The smile was clear in the voice. *Yes. Come, break your fast tomorrow at the temple. The Daughters will prepare food for you. We will look upon you, and we will give you gifts to take to the girl.*

****

Glem was unable to sleep that night. He tossed and turned. He meditated. He prayed to the Mothers. An hour before dawn he rose from his small bed roll, went out to the ocean, and bathed.

He was to go to the temple. He had never expected to leave this island, let alone go to the Isle of the Mothers and then be sent out into the world. Aside from the occasional delivery of food and necessities to the island, it had been so long since he had spoken to other people at any length, that he wasn't even sure he'd be able to hold a conversation. In fact, he realized as he washed himself that he had no desire to hold a conversation.

As the sun rose, he pushed his small boat into the water. The sea was smooth, the early sky clear. The mountains of the Isle just visible in the distance, the fog that shrouded their peaks ever present.

On the other shore, four priestesses stood awaiting him. They wore the matching robes of the Daughters. They were regal, their loose dress blowing gently in the early sea breeze. As he pulled his boat onto the sand, they approached.

"Welcome, Wise Glem. The Mothers have asked us to bring you to the temple."

He had not been called by his title 'Wise' in many years, and it sounded strange on his ears.

"Thank you, Daughters."

As they walked the small cobblestone path, the temple came into view in the brightening early light. Majestic was the only word that Glem could think of.

He paused, admiring it for a moment. Three stories high, it was built of the purest of quartz. The pillars gleaming, he was struck again by the fact that he was the first man to set eyes on this holy place in at least hundreds of years.

"Is everything well, Wise," one of the priestesses asked.

He looked at her for only a moment before resuming his walk. "Yes, I am just in awe."

The priestess smiled and nodded. "It never looses its beauty, no matter how many times you see it."

As they stepped into the temple, Glem saw that the outside paled in comparison to the inside. The interior was wide open, dark basalt tiles lined the floor. The room they entered was at least a hundred feet long, and half that in width. Pillars of the same quartz as used to build the outside stretched from floor to ceiling. The pillars were as big around as a large tree. The grooves in them lined with gold. As he followed their height to the ceiling, he was again stopped in his tracks.

Beautiful, is it not?

The voice of the Mother that he had heard before in his mind was now an echo, both in his mind and all around him. "Yes, I have never seen such beauty," he said, not removing his eyes from the ceiling.

Painted in the curves of the ceiling, extending the entire length and width of the room, were scenes of the Mothers when they had form. Great, majestic dragons flying free in the skies. Near the middle of the room, the scene turned dark. A winged demon doing battle with the Mothers, before he was imprisoned at the very back of the room.

"B'nakma," Glem said under his breath.

Yes. Once just a man, once my greatest champion. He craved more than being my most honored of champions, more than the bed he shared with me before I was a Mother. He wanted to rule.

Glem shook his head. He was beginning to feel overwhelmed. All of this, coming to the Isle, seeing the temple, speaking with a Mother. Not just a Mother, she said that B'nakma was her champion, her lover. He reached out and steadied himself on one of the pillars. "Gwimsum," he asked.

The smile clear in her voice, she confirmed her identity. *Perceptive. Yes, I was once named Gwimsum. The mother of Heekah, and the grandmother of the girl. Now, though, I am just one of the many Mothers.*

Glem knew that when the Queen of Hilcha died, she became a dragon in her next life. After the battle with B'nakma, the dragons all disappeared. Rumors spread that by defeating B'nakma, they had sacrificed themselves. But soon after, the Mothers began speaking to some of the women. The next plane of existence, it seemed, had been to become spirits.

Daughters, the voice said gently, *lead Wise Glem to the table please. He needs to rest and break his fast. Then we will speak more.*

After Glem had eaten his meal in silence, the Daughters came and removed the dishes from the table. Although the dining hall was much smaller than the main hall, it was still impressive; luxurious chairs sat at a table of dark wood. The eating utensils were polished to a silver gleam. Even the plates that he had been served his food on were made of the most delicate and posh porcelain he had ever seen. Silver and gold scrolling laced the edges of the plates.

One of the Daughters returned. "Please, follow me."

Glem stood and she led him back into the main hall. For a moment he thought she would lead him back outside, but she turned. Touching one of the side walls of the hall, the stone rumbled, then slid away. A curved staircase seemed to be cut right into the stone of the wall.

"The Mothers will speak to you upstairs. When they have finished, please show yourself back to your boat." She paused for a moment. "It has been our pleasure hosting you. We have not had visitors in some time, and the change was most exciting for us."

As the woman gracefully stepped back, the wall slid back into place. Glem climbed the stairs. At the top, a doorway opened into a spacious, yet simple room. In the middle stood a small, dark wooden table with two small boxes. The far end of the room had a small window, and the sunlight seemed to shine directly on the two boxes. The boxes were made of the same wood as the table, and inlayed with the golden symbol of a dragon.

You have served us well, Wise Glem. You have lived a simple life, and have never strayed from the oath you took to be our Wise.

"I came close, early on. Although I'm sure you are aware of that, Mother."

We are aware of all. No person is without weakness, least of all a man. The words weren't harsh, and Glem felt no offense. *But your loyalty has been admirable. We would ask one more task of you before you leave your service.*

This surprised Glem. He wasn't surprised that they would ask something of him, he was sworn to be their servant after all. No, what surprised him was that they thought he would leave their service. "I don't intend to end my service to you. True, I was only required to serve as Wise for ten years, but I have found peace and purpose in this life. I intend to serve until my days expire."

And expire they will, if you accept this task.

This gave Glem pause. "Are you saying I'll die if I do as you ask?"

Yes, the voice said gently. *You do not have to accept. Your service speaks for itself, and you will be honored with your full reward for your service. But there is no other that we trust to do this. And if you accept, you will lose your life in our service.*

Somewhere, Glem knew that he had family. He had never paired with a woman, he had never had children. But he had siblings and cousins. He had always pictured himself one day leaving his service to live out his days with the family that he no longer knew.

"And there is no one else that can do this?"

There are others. There are Wise that we will assign this to if you refuse. But there is no one that we trust, or have such confidence in, as you.

Glem had given the Mothers nearly his entire life. Now they asked for all that was left of it. "I..I would like to see my family before I am unable."

The last time you saw your family, was the last time you would see your family, Gwimsum's voice said sadly. *But, while you will never see them again no matter your choice, you can save them. You can save all of Hilcha.*

"You ask much. What is the task?"

Open the boxes.

Glem did as he was directed. The first box contained a diamond on a silver chain. The inside of the diamond seemed to move, light smoke wisping as if blown by a gentle breeze. He recognized the stone. "This is the royal diamond. The queen wears this, it's said to contain dragons' breath."

There are more than one. The queen has one, yes. As does the princess. And this one we ask that you give to the princess as well.

Glem raised an eyebrow. "The chain does not appear to be long enough to circle even a child's neck."

The voice chuckled. *Indeed, it is not. The princess is accompanied by a cat. He followed her to the other world, spent years searching for her, and this is a reward for him.*

Glem wanted to question what use a diamond collar to a cat was, but he also then wondered how a cat could have gone to the other world and found the princess. In the end, it didn't matter. This was an easy task, and he would do as the Mother's asked. "It will be done," he said, gently closing the box.

Open the other.

When Glem did, he was amazed by the craftmanship of the item inside. "It is beautiful," he said, reaching to remove it from the case.

No! Only the hands of Princess Kuin, the first of her name, may touch it.

The voice hadn't yelled, but it had so much authority to it that he pulled his hand back as if burned. He quickly closed the box. "It will be done."

Good. Bring the boxes to my granddaughter, and then train her. Stay with her for the remainder of your days, few though they will be.

"Can you tell me how I will die," Glem asked, weight now bearing on his shoulders like stones.

No. But when you do, when you fulfill your task, we will welcome you with open arms. Now go. Go and complete your task.

"It will be done," Glem said, as he gathered the two boxes and began descending the stairs. He left the Isle of the Mothers and began the final act of his life.

11

In the week since Kuin had remembered everything, she felt like she hadn't had a chance to breathe. Her parents were overjoyed to have her home, but she could see a pain in her father's eyes knowing that his son was out there somewhere. They had told her how Graystone was her father's son from before he had met her mother. She couldn't blame the man for missing his son, she too missed him dearly.

They had just finished breakfast and there was another knock on the door. Kuin looked to her parents across the table as her mother got up to answer the door. More visitors. Kuin just wanted a day to spend with her parents. A day to talk to them, to get to know them. A day to cry freely for the best friend turned brother that was out there somewhere in the hands of a dark god.

Heekah came rushing into the kitchen. "It's your cousin's guard. She will be here within the hour."

Her cousin, Briyul, was the Queen of Hilcha. After Kuin and Graystone had disappeared, her mother had stepped down from her throne. Kuin had been next in line, but with her missing Briyul stepped in.

"Can't we just have a day without someone coming to see me? I feel like a sideshow freak right now."

Her father raised his eyebrow. "A what who now?"

Kuin rolled her eyes. The other thing that had become apparent in the past week was that she had lived a very different life in a very different world. "A sideshow freak. Someone that is different so people come to gawk and gossip, point and laugh."

Heekah came and wrapped her arms around Kuin, kissing her cheek. "No one is pointing and laughing at you. You're not a 'sideshow freak'. People are just happy to know that you have returned. They want to see you. But," she said with a sigh, "after Briyul leaves, we will take some time for just us. No visitors."

Kuin gave a small smile. "Promise?"

Heekah smiled back and squeezed her daughter again. "I promise. But for now, let's get you ready for your cousin."

A half hour later two guards stood at her parent's front door, and the queen sat in their living room. "Kuin," she purred. "We are all so pleased that you have returned to us."

Kuin smiled politely. "Thank you. I'm glad to be with my parents again."

"I can only imagine," Briyul sobered. "It must have been so difficult being in an entirely different world, separated from your family. I'm sure your life was a hard one."

The queen looked at her with a look of pity that made Kuin uncomfortable. "Yes, well, all of that is behind me now."

"Yes, of course. And now that you have returned, you must come visit the capital. We would love to have you as a guest for a feast in your honor. Perhaps even a tournament to celebrate your return. You can see what it's like in the palace and see the best of what Hilcha has to offer."

Heekah touched her daughter's hand. "I'm sure that Kuin would be honored. Perhaps with time she could make the trip. Maybe even in the spring."

"The spring? Tosh! We will have her out for the fall festival. She can enjoy the end of the season at the palace. It's lovely that time of year, as I'm sure you remember."

Heekah smiled tightly. "Certainly, I remember. But the fall festival is only a couple of months away, and she would be better served coming in the spring, after the thaw."

Briyul returned the smile. "Is the princess unable to speak for herself?"

Kuin stiffened. "I certainly am. And we would love to be your guests for the fall festival. Now if you will excuse us, I'm sure it's been a long journey to come see us and it would probably be good for you to start the journey home at once."

The queen smiled. "Speak you can, indeed. Thank you for your hospitality," she said as she rose. "You are correct, it is a long journey. I look forward to seeing you again for the festival."

When the queen had left, Kuin turned on her mother. "She's right, I can speak for myself. I've spent my entire life speaking for myself, looking out for myself. I didn't have you there to make my decisions, and I don't need you to start now."

When Kuin started off to her bedroom, Heekah made to follow. A gentle hand on her arm stopped her. "Let her cool off. She has your temper. Talking to her right now will only cause a fight."

Fyan was right, of course, and she knew it. Tears filled her eyes. "I should've been there for her."

"We both should have," Fyan said, wrapping his wife in his arms. "But we didn't even know where 'there' was. We will be here for her from this day forward. But she's right, she needs space. She isn't used to anyone looking out for her."

Heekah looked up at her husband. "Graystone did. They somehow found each other. And our sweet Bo found them."

As if on cue, the white cat came and rubbed on their legs, purring loudly.

✸✸✸

Kuin lay on the comfortable bed in her room. How many nights had she dreamed she had a comfortable bed? And a comfortable bed in her parent's home, nonetheless? But she was angry. She was angry that her parents never came for her, angry that they had lived their life as if she was dead. She was angry that now that she was back, she still didn't feel like she actually had her parents. She felt more like she had two older, kind, caring foster parents. This didn't feel like home.

As Bo came in and rubbed against her before curling at her feet, her anger turned to sadness. Tears fell freely, and she knew that she wasn't mad at her parents. She was sad for what she could have had but didn't. She was scared because somewhere out there was her best friend, her brother, the one person that did actually feel like her family, in the hands of an evil and angry god.

Bo stretched and lay down on her chest, curling into a ball and purring loudly. She stroked him lovingly. "We'll figure out how to get you back to human form, but for now, thank you."

He just rubbed his head on her hand before closing his eyes. They both fell asleep.

✳✳✳

Kuin awoke to a gentle knock on her door. When she opened her eyes, the light that filtered in through the window was orange. She had slept all afternoon. "Come in," she said as she sat up in her bed.

The door opened and her mother stepped in. "Did you have a good nap?"

Kuin shrugged. "I guess. I didn't realize I had slept so long."

"May I," Heekah asked as she gestured to the edge of the bed.

Kuin scooted over with a nod and made room for the older woman. Her mother rested her hand on Kuin's. "I know that it has been a non-stop craze of emotions and visitors since you've arrived-"

"Even before I got here. Things haven't been normal for what feels like forever, I guess since Graystone got shot," Kuin interjected.

Heekah nodded. "Yes, it sounds like the two of you have had a rough few weeks."

Kuin scoffed. "Rough? You think? I'm in a world I didn't even know existed, with parents that I didn't even know existed, and the one person that I want here is being held by a god of darkness. Rough seems like a nice way to put it."

Kuin knew that she was being petulant, but she felt so lost, and being harsh seemed to be her go to defense.

Heekah nodded. "I'm sorry. I have no idea what that must feel like. I…we…your father and I," she stammered, "will do anything we can to help you get through this. Anything. We will do our best, but we can't read minds, and if you need something from us please, please ask us."

Kuin softened, a small smile pulling at the edges of her mouth. "Reading minds isn't a normal thing in Hilcha?"

Her mother laughed gently. "No, I'm afraid that is not something we can do here."

Kuin looked at the other woman for a moment, before throwing her arms around her. "I'm trying," she said as she felt tears roll freely down her cheek.

Heekah rubbed her daughters back as she had done to soothe her as a baby. "I know, sweet girl. And we will get through this."

As Kuin sobbed, her body shuddering in her mothers arms, Heekah just held her and continued rubbing her back.

12

The next morning, after breakfast, Kuin convinced her parents to let her go explore their farm alone. "I'm used to being on my own, I feel like I'm being smothered. I need to stretch my legs and be by myself for a little while."

Her parents had been reluctant, but they let her go. She walked through their small patches of crops, past a couple of buildings, and out to the woods that lined the back of the farm.

As she walked, she tried to feel Graystone. She hadn't had another vision, and she hadn't felt anything from the connection that she had only just learned they shared. She convinced herself that if he was dead, she would have felt his death. But the emptiness that she felt still ached with loss. She needed her brother.

Something rustled behind her in the trees, and a twig snapped. She spun around but didn't see anyone. She convinced herself it was just a small animal, though she realized then that she didn't know what strange types of animals they may have here, and kept walking. She hadn't left the farm since she arrived, and she had only met a handful of people. She had seen some horses, but did they have other animals that she had never seen? Hell, they have two moons, she thought. Anything is possible.

A few moments later, there was the undeniable sound of footfalls behind her, but when she spun around she again saw no one. "Who's there?"

"Please don't be afraid," a small, young voice said.

"You idiot," a slightly older voice scolded. "It's the princess, I told you not to talk to her."

"I'm not going to hurt you," she said as she reached for a thick, but not very large, stick.

"Now you've done it," the older voice hissed.

"Okay," the younger voice said, "but don't hurt us. We just wanted to see you."

As Kuin looked around for the source of the voices, she saw a pair of eyes peaking around one of the trees. No, not around the tree. The eyes were a part of the tree. She let out a small yelp as from the tree two figures appeared. They looked like they were made of tree bark, but they had a strangely human form.

"I told you we would scare her," the slightly bigger figure with the older voice said.

"I'm sorry," the young one said, kicking around some leaves with what Kuin assumed was his toe. "I didn't mean to scare you, I just wanted to meet you."

She guessed that the older one was maybe her age, and the younger one must have been half that. "What...are you," she asked hesitantly.

"Well that's damn rude," the older one said. "What do we look like? You've never seen an tree fairy before?"

"I...well...actually, no, I haven't," Kuin stammered.

"But you're the princess," the young one said, confused.

"I am, but I don't know anything about this place. I lived somewhere else my whole life."

The older fairy cocked their head. "Where were you? Everyone knows that you disappeared, but everyone also thought you were dead."

Blunt, Kuin thought. "I was taken to another world. What's your name?"

"Gungdilkew," the older fairy answered. "And this is my brother, Chis."

Kuin thought that they both were smiling at her, but not knowing what an tree fairy's expressions looked like for sure, she couldn't know. "It's nice to meet you," she said. "I was just walking; would you like to join me?"

What she thought was a smile grew large on the face of the younger fairy, Chis. Gungdilkew on the other hand, did not seem to share his enthusiasm. "We really shouldn't. Just talking to you is dangerous enough, if you told your guard..." they trailed off before finishing.

"Dangerous how? And I don't have a guard," Kuin said, instantly regretting that she had said the latter part. What if they were waiting to hurt her, checking to see if she was alone, and now she just confirmed to them that it was just her. "Though my family will be right behind me," she lied.

Kuin regretted the lie when both fairies began looking around anxiously, Chis's whole body shaking, his leaves rustling nervously. "But it's okay, they won't care if we hang out."

Chis whirled to their sibling. "She wants to hang us," fear making his small voice tremble.

"We're sorry to have bothered you, your highness. Forgive us," Gungdilkew said, reaching their branches out and wrapping them around Chis's. Before she could speak, they disappeared into the woods.

****

When she returned home, Heekah and Fyan were sitting on the porch, a pipe in both of their hands.

Heekah nearly leapt from her seat when she saw Kuin approaching. "How was your walk?"

"Good, I think. Certainly educational."

"Educational? How so," her father asked, taking a drag from his pipe.

"When did you plan to tell me there were fairies here?"

Fyan coughed and choked on his pipe as he stood, looking around anxiously.

"Where, where are there fairies? And how many," Heekah asked. She too was looking around as if there was danger.

"Two, there were two in the woods. They were just kids, I think," Kuin said. "What is wrong with fairies?"

Fyan spit at the ground. "They are murderous, blood thirsty creatures," he spat.

"Some are," Heekah said, giving her husband a sharp look. "Just because some are, does not mean that you can condemn them all."

"Your niece did, and that's why they are dangerous."

"Briyul is an idiot, yes, but just because they were banished, does not make them dangerous."

"Hey, can someone please explain what the hell you're talking about," Kuin cut in.

"Language," both parents said at the same time, turning to look at her.

Kuin put her hands up. "Fine, but can you please explain?"

Heekah sighed. "There was a time that all of the species of Hilcha lived in harmony. Not perfection, there were fights, even some larger skirmishes. But we lived side by side, and we did so for generations. But when you were taken, and I stepped down..."

"The other species saw an opportunity. And they tried to take it," Fyan finished.

"They seemed nice, and they didn't try to hurt me at all. And what do you mean by other species," Kuin asked.

"I know that the world you were raised on only had humans," Fyan started.

"I mean, we have all kinds of animals on Earth. It's not just humans."

Fyan nodded. "Yes, but we're not talking about animals. We are talking about other civilized species. Species that have their own systems of hierarchy, that speak, that love."

"Animals can love," Kuin started, but her father cut her off.

"You know what I mean. It's not just fairies."

"Okay, so like, what then?"

"The fairies as you know. Mers. Centaurs. Elves. An occasional troll, though those have not been seen in a very long time. And of course, the dragons, though no one has seen them in a very long time. But they stay on the island."

"Dragons," Kuin asked, her eyebrows raising.

"Of course," Heekah answered. "The mothers of our royal bloodline, when they die, they become one of the Mothers, one of the dragons that protect our land. They are the ones that forced B'nakma into submission all those years ago. All of Hilcha fought beside them, but without their power we would have all fallen."

"But now he's back, and Hilcha stands divided?"

Kuin's mother sighed. "Yes. After you and Graystone disappeared, I couldn't fulfill my duties as queen. I was lost. For years I was lost. I stepped away, and Briyul stepped in as next in line. The peace and unity that held over Hilcha between all of her inhabitants faltered. It has never been the same."

"So, humans are at war with the fairies?"

Fyan spat on the ground again. "We should be, they are violent creatures, and Briyul believed that they were involved in you and your brother's disappearance. But no," her father shook his head, "we are not at war. Just fights wherever humans' cross paths with the other people of the world."

When Kuin scoffed and shook her head, her mother raised her eyebrow. "What?"

"It would seem that humans are violent, divisive creatures no matter the world."

It was Heekah's turn to scoff. "We became 'divisive' because you were stolen and the other creatures were the ones that took the two of you."

"Were they," Kuin asked, her voice rising. "You know, on Earth, Graystone is viewed as less than by many other humans because his skin is darker than theirs. For generations, people that look like him were enslaved to labor for people that look like us. People that looked like him were beaten, tortured, raped, and killed just because they were seen as different and 'less than'. Do you have proof that the other people of Hilcha had anything to do with our being taken?"

Her parents both shook their heads. "But-", her father started.

"Save it," Kuin said, turning and leaving the porch.

"Where are you going," her mother called after her.

"I need some space," she called over her shoulder, not stopping.

"It's getting dark, you can go out tomorrow," Fyan said, moving to follow her.

Kuin whirled. "I will decide when and where I go. Just because you are my mother and father in title does not give you authority over me. I have lived my entire damned life without you telling me what to do, and that doesn't change now."

When Kuin turned to continue walking, her father grabbed her arm. Not harshly, it didn't hurt, but it infuriated Kuin. "Don't touch me," she yelled, shoving her father back. When she shoved him, he flew through the air, landing about ten feet away. Her hand felt warm, and she thought she could see smoke or steam rising from it.

Fyan looked at her with wide eyes. "Please, don't go right now. We need to talk. You're powers are starting, you can't go now."

Kuin walked away without another word.

13

"Gungdilkew," Kuin called out as she walked through the woods she had been in earlier. "Chis. Are you guys around?"

No answer.

"I don't want to hurt you. I think you misunderstood me earlier. I am not my family, and I just want to learn and get to know you."

No answer.

"Please," Kuin asked, her voice cracking ever so slightly. She felt so alone, and she wanted to talk to someone that wasn't trying to tell her what to do.

"You wanted to hang us," came a voice from off to her side somewhere.

Kuin turned to the voice, but she saw no one. "No," she shook her head. "Where I'm from 'hang out' just means to spend time with someone. Just kind of doing nothing, just…I don't know, hanging out."

Chis's small face came from a tree startlingly close to her. "You don't want to kill us?"

"No, of course not."

"Now you've done it," said Gungdilkew, smacking their brother on the back of the head. They turned their gaze to Kuin. "You may not want to kill us, but those like you do. I can fight for myself, and I don't fear any human. But my brother is far too small. They would pull his branches off and throw him into one of their fires."

Kuin took a step back. "I would never do that to you, or him, or anyone. Is that something that humans have done to you?"

Gungdilkew scoffed. "That is the nicest way that they kill us."

Kuin shook her head. "Well, I'm not like them, and I'm not from here. And I don't think all humans want to kill you."

"Perhaps. But my brother's life is not something I'm willing to risk. But we will walk with you here if you would like. You certainly aren't any threat to me."

Chis released the tree that he had clung to and hopped down by Kuin's feet. This close, he was even smaller than she had thought. His tallest sprout on top of his head only came to her knee. "You won't hurt us," he asked with a hopeful smile.

Kuin knelt down so she could look him in his eyes. "No, I will never hurt you," she said with a warm smile of her own.

She was surprised when he grabbed her hand with one of his branches. "Let's go then, we can show you our home!"

While Gungdilkew seemed less than thrilled about the idea, he followed behind them, mumbling something about 'humans'.

"Are your parents home? Will they be upset if you bring me," Kuin asked.

"Our parents are dead," Gungdilkew answered sharply from behind her.

"I'm sorry. I know what it's like to grow up without parents," Kuin said quietly.

"Do you know what it's like to have your parents murdered right in front of you? To watch them be chopped apart by the swords of man?"

Kuin shook her head, and she felt Chis's hand tighten around hers. "Not all humans are bad, you said that yourself," he said to his brother.

"No, they are not. But it was her cousin's men that did it. So forgive me if I'm not gentle when I speak of it."

"I am not the queen, and I would never do that. But I do apologize for the terrible acts of the humans. My world, or the world I grew up on rather, is very different than this one, and yet so very alike in many ways it would seem."

"Oh, we're almost there," Chis said excitedly, pulling her along faster.

When he stopped suddenly, Kuin thought something was wrong. "What is it? I thought we were going to your home?"

Chis giggled like the small child he was. "We are here, silly."

"There's nothing here," Kuin said, looking around.

"Ha! Imagine that: a human that can't see the world that is right in front of them."

Kuin was going to say something witty to Gungdilkew, but she found herself unable to speak when they raised their hand and the trees parted. What lay beyond was a beautiful home of sticks and leaves, flowers and vines. Two stories high, the house was circular, almost like a lighthouse from earth.

Chis tugged on her hand. "Do you like it?"

Kuin smiled broadly. "I love it. It is beautiful. It's like something out of a fairy tale."

Chis cocked his head to the side. "We don't tell tales about simple homes like ours."

Kuin's smile deepened somehow. "I'm sorry, it's an expression from earth. We don't have fairies on earth, so a 'fairy tale' describes a fanciful tale that is far too amazing to be true."

Chis just shrugged, at least that's what Kuin thought it was. "I'm glad you like it. Come on, I'll show you around!"

Chis showed Kuin around their home excitedly. They had no need for a kitchen, because they didn't cook anything. Apparently, tree fairies only ate raw foods. They had a spacious living area, complete with a couch of sorts. Vines and branches were woven together and topped with soft moss. She was surprised to find it was one of the more comfortable couches she had sat on, though most of her life she hadn't had a couch of any kind.

"Come on," Chis said excitedly, pulling her hand. He led her up the stairs, and to a room full of what appeared to be toys. Balls of twigs beautifully woven together, dolls made from sticks with what she thought were mushrooms for eyes.

"This is beautiful," she said, looking around the room.

"Nothing compared to your palace, I'm sure," Gungdilkew said grumpily. They apparently weren't as excited to have her visiting as Chis was.

"I wouldn't know, I don't have a palace. I've never even seen the palace, and the one palace I have seen," she said, thinking of the Palace Theatre from what felt like a lifetime ago, "it is nothing compared to this. You seem to forget, this may be where I was born, but this has never been my home."

Seemingly rebuked, they lowered their head. "You're right. There are just many things that make our kind fear humans, especially one of the royal family."

Kuin touch their arm gently. "I may be from the royal family, but you have nothing to fear from me. I only want to learn about this world and figure out how to get my brother back."

While Chis began playing with his toys, Gungdilkew sat down on a small bench that ran the length of the room. Kuin sat down beside them.

"I'm sorry," they said. "I know that you are not a normal, spoiled royal. But we have lived in fear for far too long. And I guess my prejudices are stronger than I'd care to admit. Please, tell me about your brother."

Kuin sat back against the wall and did. She told them all about how he had come into her life in the other world, how he had become her best friend, how he had protected her. She told them how he had been hurt in their world, and how he had healed so quickly. "The crazy part is, I know that he is my brother now. But I don't think he does. I haven't seen him since we got here."

"B'nakma has him," Gungdilkew said flatly.

"Yes."

"He will use Graystone's body to take human form. And when he does," they paused. "When he does, he will take Hilcha as his own. And as scary as it has been will pale in comparison to what will be then."

"Graystone will fight," Kuin said, trying to sound strong but knowing her voice waivered.

"Undoubtedly. But if what you say is true about how quick he recovered from his injuries on…Arth?"

"Earth," she corrected.

"Earth," they said with a nod. "Given how quick he recovered, it is my guess that he has already given himself to B'nakma."

Kuin sat up straight. "What do you mean?"

"B'nakma needed a strong body, and your father is a known strong and fierce warrior. His bloodline would be strong enough to handle a God pouring their magic into his body. And I would guess that he either took Graystone's body when he was weak, though from what I've heard from the elders that is not possible, or more likely Graystone gave it to him willingly."

"No, he wouldn't do that," she said, shaking her head emphatically. She told them about her vision of Graystone leaping from the tower and B'nakma catching him.

Gungdilkew rested their hand over Kuin's. "Well, no matter how, B'nakma has him in the forbidden mountains, and likely has already taken his body. He is now just trying to strengthen enough to wage war. When he is strong, none will stand."

Kuin didn't know what to say. She sat back against the wall again and closed her eyes. No, she thought, there is no way that her brother was gone and B'nakma now controlled him. He was still there. She would save him.

"Come Chis, it's time for bed," Gungdilkew said, taking Kuin from her thoughts.

"Can Princess Kuin tuck me in," the young fairy asked with a pleading expression.

"Only if you don't call me princess again," she said with a small but genuine smile. The innocent child in front of her warmed her heart in a way that helped ease the pain of her brother being missing.

After they tucked Chis into bed, Gungdilkew offered Kuin some tea in the living room. "We don't have much that you would be able to, or want to for that matter, eat. But I can make tea. Everyone loves tea.”

Kuin smiled. “I’ve never really drank tea, but sure, I could use something to drink.”

A few moments later, they sat next to each other on the couch. Kuin pulled her legs underneath her and sipped the tea. It was delightfully sweet, and very relaxing. “I wish I had some of this to drink before bed.”

“Speaking of,” Gungdilkew said, setting their tea down on the arm of the couch, “shouldn’t you get home before your parents worry about you.”

“I’m sure they already are. They shouldn’t have treated me like a child. I can handle myself.”

“But, you are a child, and you may be able to handle yourself where you are from, but this is not Earth. Hilcha can be very dangerous, especially with B’nakma returning. His demons prowl now more than ever, and much farther south than ever before. Even almost here to the wood.”

Kuin looked at them. “Are you a danger to me?”

Gungdilkew smiled. “No, I am not. But your parents may think otherwise.”

“Their problem,” she said with a small shrug, and laid her head on Gungdilkew’s shoulder.

They moved slightly, and she lifted her head. “I’m sorry. I didn’t mean to invade your personal space,” she said, her cheeks darkening just a little.

“Not at all,” they chuckled. “I just thought, if you were going to rest on me, perhaps you would prefer this form.”

Gungdilkew stood, and transformed before her. Their branches and leaves were turned into dark green skin. They had a small skirt of flowers, and their bare chest was covered with thin moss.

"Whoa, what, how, wait," Kuin stammered.

"This is how we normally look when we go out in the world. It's more," they paused, looking for the right word. "Palatable for humans. More like what you are used to."

"You look very handsome, quite the man."

"I am not a man. I am a fairy. And I don't feel like I'm a 'he', nor a 'she' really. I find many of the qualities of the male and female gender's to be appealing. I am also attracted to many different species and genders. So I live my life how I want to, I don't care what others think of me. I just am."

Kuin nodded. "What do others call you?"

Gungdilkew scrunched up their nose. "Gungdilkew, if they aren't calling me a monster."

Kuin chuckled. "No, like, 'he is very handsome'," she clarified, "or 'she is very pretty'."

"Oh. Everyone calls me they. Or them."

They sat back down on the couch. "Now, if you would like to rest your head, you wont have any sticks poking your eye," they chuckled.

Kuin smiled at Gungdilkew and put her head back on their shoulder. She had to admit, they were more comfortable this way. She closed her eyes and fell asleep.

14

"Go away," Kuin mumbled, rolling over and wrapping her blanket tighter around herself.

"Princess, Princess, wake up, they're here!"

When Kuin heard the fear in Chis's voice, and felt his frantic tugging on her hand, she sat up alert. "What's wrong? Who's here?"

"The humans," Chis said, shuddering.

"What humans? Where is Gungdilkew?"

"He heard them enter the wood. He went to see what they wanted, and they caught him. They're hurting him," Chis nearly whimpered.

"Which way," Kuin asked, racing out of the door.

Chis grabbed her hand. "I'll show you."

Kuin turned to him and knelt down to look him in the eyes. "No, just point me which way. You have to stay here."

Chis scrunched up his face. "I'm brave! I can help."

Kuin squeezed his hand. "I know, and that is why you have to stay here and make sure your home is safe. Hide it like it was when I first got here and stay inside until your sibling or I return. Can you do that for me?"

Chis straightened, clearly proud of getting such an important assignment. "Yes!"

"Good, now which way?"

Chis pointed the way that she had come with them to get to the house. "Okay," she said. "Now go inside and hide unless it is me or Gungdilkew that comes."

Kuin ran for only a moment before she heard shouting. She heard Gungdilkew shriek in what she thought sounded like pain. A second later she entered a small clearing. "Stop," she yelled.

Her father and her mother both spun to look at her, and Gungdilkew sagged to the ground. He looked like he was…bleeding? Do trees bleed? All around were branches that Kuin soon realized came from them. They had been tortured by her parents.

"Stay back," Heekah called out. "He is still dangerous."

"Dangerous? Gungdilkew? And they aren't a 'he'," she said, rushing to their side.

"Kuin, you need to get back," her father said, taking a step toward her.

She stood, back straight. "No, they are my friend, and you need to leave."

Fyan scoffed. "Fairies are friends to no one," he said as he continued to walk towards her. "And with your powers awakening, they will try to use you."

"Use me? The only one's that have tried to use me so far are humans. And my powers? What powers? Did you think that maybe you should have told me about these powers?"

"We didn't know that they were awakening until you threw your father back at the house. Please, come with us and we can help you understand," her mother nearly pleaded.

Kuin shook her head. "No. Leave, please. I'll come back when I'm ready. But I'm going to help my friend heal from what you did to them, and no one is going to stop me."

Fyan started to argue more, but Bo came out of the trees behind Kuin. He rubbed his head on her leg, and then began licking Gungdilkew's wounds.

"I think he's trying to tell you something," Kuin said to her parents. "He protected me and Graystone on earth when we were attacked. He's here now, and he sure looks like he's trying to tell you to leave me to help my friend."

Before her father could say anything, Heekah put a hand on his shoulder. "Come on, we need to go."

Fyan pointed a finger at Gungdilkew. "If she doesn't return, I will come back to these woods and burn every last tree."

Kuin watched as her parents walked away, speechless that they could do and say what they just did.

"Can you walk," she asked Gungdilkew, reaching down to try to help them stand.

"Yes," they answered.

They walked back to the home in silence, Bo following.

****

"How could they do this," Kuin asked as she sat with Gungdilkew on the couch.

"Fear," they answered. "Fear of me, of fairies, and fear for you."

Their wounds had already started to heal, branches growing back where the old ones had been torn off.

"That's crap," Kuin said. "Fear is not a good reason to hurt another person."

They smiled. "To them, I am not a person. I am a creature. A monster. To be fair, if I thought that someone was a danger to Chis, I would likely do the same. They were not trying to kill me. Only get me to tell them where you were."

"Why didn't you?"

"Because I get the feeling that you did not want them to know. And, more importantly," he sighed, "because I couldn't let them find Chis."

"Thank you," was all Kuin said as she hugged them gently.

Chis's voice came from the stairs. "They're going to kill us, aren't they," he asked quietly.

Kuin went over to him, and picked him up. He felt light, and he wrapped his branches around her neck in a hug. "No," she said, "I promise, I will not let them hurt you or your sibling again. I may not know what things are like here, but this is not okay on any world."

Chis just said "Okay," and buried his face into her shoulder.

She sat on the couch, holding Chis. Gungdilkew rested against her comfortably, and Bo curled on the armrest next to her.

"What powers do they think I have?"

She had expected to Gungdilkew to answer, but it was Chis that surprised her.

"The power of the Mothers. You will be one of them one day, and until you pass into Motherhood, you still have some of the power. At least, that's what everyone says."

"The Mothers?"

Chis pulled his head back from her shoulder and turned so that he was sitting on her lap. "You really don't know," he asked, eyes wide.

Kuin just shook her head.

"Oh dear. I'm just a kid and even I know the Mothers. Dragons. Your family, the Royal family, you are dragons."

Kuin blinked. "Dragons? Like wings and fire?"

Chis nodded excitedly. "Yes, though no one has seen them since they battled B'nakma and locked him away. Some people think they all died saving Hilcha, others say that they hide on their isle because they aren't needed."

"Wait, my family are dragons? And they are the ones that locked up B'nakma?"

"Of course," Chis said, his tone as if he were speaking to a child. "Who else would've saved us?"

"You young sir, are just a child," she said gently squeezing his nose, "don't talk to me like I'm the child."

"But, you kind of seem like you are," he shrugged.

"Okay, so let me make sure I understand this: You think that I am a dragon? And that I have some sort of powers because I'm a dragon?"

Chis nodded with a big, innocent smile. "Yes, that's exactly it. You can save us. That's why you're here. Probably why you were taken in the first place really. Can't stop B'nakma if you aren't here. But, now that he's gotten stronger, he needed a body and your brother-"

"Graystone," Kuin cut in, tired of him just being called her 'brother'.

"And Graystone," Chis continued, "was the ideal host. So B'nakma had to come for him."

"I don't know anything about my powers, if they're even real," she said doubtfully. "And so I certainly can't save anyone."

"They're real," Gungdilkew said. "What you did when you threw your father shows that they are there.

They just need…awakened? Trained? Developed? I don't know, but they are there."

"My father," she said, shaking her head. "All of my life, I wondered what it would be like to have a family. Now I have one, and I've ruined it with them."

"No," they said. "Trust me. Your mother and father never let go of the hope of seeing you again one day. They just have to accept that you aren't the baby they remembered, and you have to understand that they don't know how to be parents to an adolescent girl."

Kuin chuckled. "Are you saying that I'm difficult because I'm a teenager?"

Gungdilkew shrugged. "That is universal, no matter the species."

"I have to go back to them. I need to make this right, and I need them to help me, teach me, about my powers."

They nodded. "Yes. But, Princess, please do me, do Hilcha, one favor?"

"Anything," she said without hesitation.

"When you have learned all of who you are, when you have control over your powers, when you sit on your family's throne, stop the hate. Stop the separation of humans from the rest of Hilcha. We have lived together for so long, and this hate and division is so very unhealthy for us all. We have all lost friends, and even some have lost family, because of the decree separating us. People were forced to choose between spouses, even between their own children, and their species. And we will all be needed to fight together if B'nakma regains his full strength."

Kuin reached out and touched their cheek gently. "You have my word."

✳✳✳

Kuin walked home, wondering, worrying, anxious at how her parents would receive her. She knew Gungdilkew was probably right, but that didn't change her apprehension. When she got close enough to the house, she could see her father pacing back and forth on the porch, pipe puffing heavily. Her mother sat in a wooden rocking chair, her own pipe much calmer.

When her mother stood and pointed at Kuin, her father ran from the porch to her. When he got to her, he wrapped her in his arms and cried. No words, no meanness, just tears. "I love you," he finally said, pulling away from her and holding her arms.

When she looked at him, she realized that her own eyes were blurry as well. How long had she wanted a father to say that? Soon her mother was there, taking her from her father's arms and hugging her close.

Kuin was about to say something, she wasn't sure what, maybe offer some sort of an apology. But before she could, her body went rigid and her eyes glossed over.

"The child's powers awaken. She must be trained. One comes to help her, do not stop him. The future of our world depends on this child. The fate of one, or the future of all."

She fell weakly into her mother's arms; she did not remember being carried into the house and laid in her bed.

* * *

15

Kuin woke in her bed, the sun long set. As she walked quietly towards the kitchen, her stomach rumbling, she heard her parents.

"It has to be the Mothers," Heekah said. "Who would they send to train her? Why can't we train her? My mother trained me."

"If it is the Mothers, then we need to do what they ask," Fyan answered.

"What do you mean if?"

"I mean, no one has seen or heard from the Mothers in generations. What if it is B'nakma? What if he sends one of his demons or shades or other creatures to corrupt her?"

Kuin walked into the kitchen. "I am not a pawn. I will not be corrupted, and I will decide if, and with whom, I will train."

"Sweetheart, sit," her mother said, pulling a stool out for her. "There is still some dinner I'll start a fire and warm it."

Kuin sat. "Thank you. Why didn't you tell me I had powers? Or about the Mothers?"

"We should have," her father admitted. "But there was, is, so much for you to learn and you seem so overwhelmed. I suppose we also wanted to protect your innocence."

"I'm fine. I need to know what to do, and how to do it, to get back Graystone."

Fyan sighed. "Yes, if we can."

"If we can," Kuin snapped the question. "We will. When you weren't there, Graystone was. My brother has protected me for years, and I'll be damned if I don't fight to get him back. He would do it for me," she said the last part with quiet sadness.

Fyan came around the table and touched her shoulder. "You're right. And I'm so sorry that we weren't there. But if B'nakma has him, who knows if Graystone is still alive, if he is still in the body he once had."

"Well, there is only one way to know," she said. "And it's not your fault that you weren't there. I'm sorry I said that. But I'm not a child anymore. I survived for years on my own, and me and Graystone did just fine."

Her mother nodded. "Yes. To us you are still just a child. We may not be able to let that go so quickly, but we will try," she said with a glance at her husband. "But we don't want you to just survive. We want you to live. To be healthy, happy, have a family, grow old."

Kuin shrugged. "You've heard the words: 'the fate of one, or the future of all'. I may not be meant to grow old. But coming here, seeing Hilcha, meeting Gungdilkew and Chis-"

Her father snorted, cutting her off.

"They are my friends," she nearly growled. "And it sounds like Hilcha once lived in unity, so stop acting like they don't deserve to live just like humans."

"Fairies, mers, and who knows what other species helped B'nakma take you and your brother from here. I'll be damned if I forget that."

"Even if that's true, my friends didn't help B'nakma. And I'd guess that more than one human aided him as well," she said, strength in her voice. "No, if returning has shown me anything, it is that someone needs to lead and heal this world. If the Mothers think that person is me, then I will decide if they are right when I learn more."

"You're right," Fyan said, lowering his head. "I am sorry. Not all fairies are bad, and not all humans are good. I should not have hurt your friend, and one day I may even get to apologize to them for what I did, but for now we have to focus. We need you to learn about who you are, and what you can do. And we need to let you be yourself, because I have no doubt that you are the same beautiful person that I helped bring into this world all those years ago. I know that you are smart, and strong, and resourceful."

"Okay," was the only response that Kuin could offer. She wasn't the 'same beautiful person' that she had been when they knew her. She was only a baby then. Now she was a person with a personality, beliefs, and convictions.

"Are you hungry," her mother asked.

"I could eat," Kuin answered with a smirk.

"Then let's eat," her father said with a big smile.

As Kuin the first bite of her dinner in her mouth, there was a strong knock on the door.

Glem had been traveling for almost two days. His feet were tired, and if not for the man that had let him ride in the back of his cart for the last few hours, he wasn't sure that he would have even made it that day.

Glem approached the house. There was a light coming from one of the rooms near the back, but otherwise it looked quiet.

When he knocked at the door, he heard a girls raised voice. "Another visitor? And at this time of night?"

A moment later a man opened the door. "Yes," the bald man asked.

"I am Wise Glem, servant of the Mothers."

The man that had answered the door just looked at him.

Glem cleared his throat. "Yes, well, I have been sent here by the Mothers with gifts for the Princess."

Before he could finish, he was floating a few inches off of the ground. His arms held down by his sides by an invisible force. "How do we know you are who you claim to be," a woman asked, appearing from behind the man.

"I have no reason to lie to you, and I have the seal of the Mothers in my pocket, Your Majesty."

Heekah released the man. "I'm not the queen."

"Once our Queen, always our Queen," Glem said, bowing low.

"What do you want," Fyan asked.

"As I said, I have gifts for Princess Kuin, the first of her name, from the Mothers. I would very much like to meet her."

"Your seal," Fyan said, holding out his hand.

As Glem fumbled in his pocket, Bo came out and rubbed against his leg.

"If Bo trusts him, that's good enough for me," Kuin said, squeezing past her parents.

"Your Royal Highness," Glem said, bowing low again.

"Um, yeah, sure. Stand up. Come in," Kuin said, ushering the man in.

"Would you like some food or water," Heekah asked as they led their visitor into the kitchen.

"It has been a long journey, Ma'am, I would be grateful for anything you can offer."

"We have plenty, sit and I'll grab something. Just don't call me 'ma'am' again. My name is Heekah."

Glem sat straight backed on one of the stools in the kitchen. "Of course, but it would not be appropriate for me to address you by name, Ma'am. You are royalty, and a future Mother."

Heekah sighed and brought him a plate of food and a glass of water, setting it next to a napkin with a fork. There was no point in arguing, the man would call her what he pleased.

"Why did the Mothers send you," Kuin asked as he began eating.

"They sent me to train you, and they wanted me to give you these," he said, putting down his fork and retrieving the two wooden boxes from his small tuck before resuming his meal.

"They are beautiful," Kuin said as she ran her hand over them. She opened the smaller box first. Inside was a necklace like hers, though with a smaller chain.

"A Royal stone," Heekah asked.

Glem nodded as he wiped his mouth on the napkin. "For the cat, they said he served your family well and they wished to reward him."

Bo appeared as if on cue. Kuin pulled the small collar from the box and put it around his neck.

Well, it's not heavy at least. What the hell do I need a fancy collar for though?

Kuin looked in amazement at the cat. She had just heard the voice of the man Robert in her mind. "Because it's quite dashing," she answered.

Bo's head snapped up to her. *You can hear me?*

"As can I," Heekah said with a small laugh. "Any who wear this stone can, although I assume only if they are near to you."

Holy hell, was all Bo said, looking from Heekah to Kuin and back again.

Heekah kneeled and rubbed his head. "Oh, sweet, sweet Bo, thank you for bringing our girl home."

Bo purred softly as she rubbed him. *Graystone is here too. I carried him into the portal on Earth. He was gone when we came through, and I was a cat once again.*

"We'll find him," Kuin said.

"Graystone," her father asked.

Kuin nodded.

Fyan knelt down picked up the cat. "Thank you," he said as his eyes began to water.

Tell him he is welcome, but please put me down. I do not like to be held, Bo said, squirming.

"Alright," Fyan said, setting the cat back down.

"You can hear him," Kuin asked, amazed.

Fyan chuckled and shook his head. "No, but I could tell what he was thinking. He's never been one to be picked up."

And yet they do, Bo sighed.

Kuin and Heekah both laughed at the cat.

"What is in the second box," Fyan asked.

Kuin opened it. Inside was a beautifully crafted knife. A gleaming black blade, carved with symbols of dragons leading to a hilt of shining silver. At the top of the hilt was a stone. "Is that a diamond," Kuin asked.

Before Glem could stop her, Heekah reached for the blade. Kuin's body went rigid. "Do not touch the dagger. Only the hands of the Princess may grace it. Without her magic, it will kill any who touch it. Train the girl, you her parents, and he, our Wise. Bring her to us in two months' time. Only the five of you. The time comes quickly now. The fate of one, or the future of all."

Kuin sank to the floor, but this time she did not faint. She sat herself up, reaching for the dagger. When she grabbed it, it felt warm in her hand and the dragons carved into the blade began to glow a bright red. The stone at the end became cloudy, as if filled with smoke. She put it back in its box and it returned to its previous state.

"A Dnif," her mother said, with wonder in her eyes. "All women in the Royal line are given one, but I've never seen one like this, nor have I ever seen one that comes directly from the Mothers. They are usually just ceremonial and have no magic."

Kuin closed the box. "I need to rest. I want to train tomorrow."

"Wise Glem, you may stay in our guest room. I will help you get settled while Heekah assists Kuin," Fyan said, leading the other man from the kitchen.

16

The next morning Kuin awoke to the sound of someone knocking on her door.

"Come in," she answered, pulling the blankets around herself.

"Your Royal Highness," a far too chipper Glem said, "the hour is late, and we have much to do. I will meet you outside in ten minutes. That should give you time to eat a quick breakfast."

Kuin sat up. "Ten minutes? You just woke me up! What time is it?"

"An hour before sunrise."

Kuin groaned and lay back down, pulling the covers over her head. "Come back when the sun is up."

"Ten minutes, Princess."

When Kuin heard the sound of the door closing, she sat up again. They couldn't have slept for more a than couple of hours. This man must be crazy to think that she could be up and ready to train so early.

Fifteen minutes later she walked out the front door and almost directly into an impatient-looking Glem.

"You're late. We must get started on time in the future."

"What happened to all of the 'your royal highness' stuff," Kuin mumbled through a bite of an apple.

Glem smacked the apple from her hand. "I have the utmost respect for you, Princess. However, I have been tasked by the Mothers with training you, and I do not wish to be a disappointment to them. You should not either. They come first, and unless they tell me to handle you with kid friendly gloves, I will train you how I see fit."

Kuin stood there in disbelief. "That was my breakfast," she managed.

"Tomorrow get up early enough to eat a proper breakfast, and you won't have to worry about missing it."

"I didn't 'miss it', you ruined it."

Glem sighed. "Your Royal Highness, I have lived in peace and solitude for decades. I do not even like children. I am here because it is the will of the Mothers. I suggest that you take this seriously. Or, if you would prefer, we can leave Graystone in the hands of a dark god and you can sleep in, cuddled up in your warm bed."

At the mention of her brother's name, Kuin glared at him. "Fine. What are we doing?"

"I'm glad you asked. It's nice to see you so interested. I want you to lift that," the Wise said, pointing to a large boulder near the road.

Kuin scoffed. "I'm afraid I'm not that strong," she said, even as she walked to it.

"You threw your father across the lawn like he weighed nothing at all, did you not?"

Kuin cringed at the memory. "Yeah, I suppose I did. But I don't know how. I just meant to push him away from me."

"Ah yes, the 'how' of it is why we are here. You have the power of the dragon in you, Princess. Under normal circumstances you would have already been trained. Unfortunately, these are not normal circumstances. The other world made you soft, kept your power dormant. Hilcha has awoken this power, and now you need to learn much in little time."

Kuin bent down and wrapped her arms around the stone. They didn't even go halfway around it. She lifted and grunted, pulled and pushed, and the rock didn't move. "This is stupid."

"Well, when Yaswi confronts you again, you can just tell her learning how to use your power was 'stupid', and I'm sure she'll just let you go," Glem said with a smirk.

Kuin glared at him. She wrestled with the boulder again, her hands slipping and falling flat on her butt.

"Now is not the time to sit."

"Then teach me what the hell I'm supposed to do. Isn't that your job?"

Glem smiled. "It is. And I told you what to do: lift the boulder."

Kuin stood up and kicked the boulder. It shifted slightly before rocking back into place. "Holy crap, did you see that?"

"I did. You kicked it. I said lift it."

Kuin tried again and again, the sky turning orange with the rising sun, and again and again the stone didn't move.

Glem sighed. "When you threw your father, was it difficult?"

Kuin matched his exasperated sigh. "No, I told you, I didn't try."

"So you didn't think about it? You didn't focus on the idea of launching him through the air?"

Kuin looked as if her temper would explode. "Very well," Glem said. "So my point is, you weren't trying to throw your father. You just did. So don't try to move the boulder, just do."

"You're a crap teacher."

Glem chuckled. "I am not a teacher. I am a Wise. Servant to the Mothers, and the assignment they have given me is to train you, and I will do so to the best of my ability."

Kuin simply shook her head and tried to move the boulder again. Huffing she stood up and threw her hands up in resignation. "I can't."

Glem nodded. "Very well. Then just forget about your brother that you claim to love. Hell, forget about everyone here. Your parents, your people, Bo. Since you 'can't' be bothered to-"

Kuin roared with anger and picked up the boulder, launching it through the air. It landed squarely in the middle of her parents' front porch, wood splintering in every direction.

As her parents came running, Kuin just stood there gobsmacked.

"What happened," her father practically shrieked, running to her. "Are you okay?"

Her mother smiled. "She seems to have gotten angry and destroyed our porch."

Glem grinned. "Yes, it took her long enough. Actually, she seems to have a rather large amount of patience."

Kuin whirled on the man. "You did this on purpose?"

Glem shrugged. "I am here to teach you, and consider this your first lesson. You have the Dragon in you. Anger is strong among the dragons, and it is powerful. Now you must learn to control that anger. Get mad, get angry, and use the power, don't let the power use you. It is a tool and you are the one holding it."

"Power isn't her only tool," her mother said, putting her arm around Kuin and looking in her eyes. "Family is the true source of our strength. Anger unlocks the door, but why you open that door is the most important part."

"She's right," Glem agreed. "If you don't control the anger, or if you use the anger for vain or petty things, you become no better than B'nakma. Your motivation, your heart, will determine what type of a ruler you will be."

"Ruler? I'm not here to rule. I don't want to rule, Hilcha has a queen. I just want Graystone back."

"Be that as it may, you are the Princess, you are next in line for the throne, and one day the crown will most certainly rest on your head."

Kuin thought about Glem's words. She didn't point out that the prophesy was clear, 'the fate of one, or the future of all', and she would likely never have to be anything more than a girl trying to save her brother.

"We'll see," she said turning to her father, "but for now, how do I fix your porch?"

"Our porch," her father corrected. "And that may be a question better asked of your mother and Wise Glem."

Heekah smiled. "Like I said, strength isn't your only tool. For now, leave the porch. Continue to do as the Wise asks. When you are ready, we will fix the porch together."

Kuin didn't look terribly pleased, but she accepted her mother's direction. "Perhaps we should do something that isn't going to endanger people or property?"

"Indeed. Let's go for a walk," Glem said, starting away from her before she could answer.

Twenty minutes later Kuin found herself in the woods where she had first met Gungdilkew and Chis. She hoped that they wouldn't think she was bringing a human to them, and at the same time wanted very much to see her friends.

"You may show yourselves; I assure you I mean you no harm. I am Glem, Wise of the Mothers, and I would like to meet you."

Kuin was delighted to her Chis' small voice answer. "Are you really a Wise?"

"Now you've done it. You always get us into trouble," came Gungdilkew's less than excited response.

Glem chuckled and stooped down as Chis came out of hiding. "I am, and the Mothers sent me to help your friend learn how to use her power."

"You're going to teach her how to be a Dragon," Chis asked, his broad smile showing his delight.

"If she will learn, yes."

"She will learn."

Kuin was surprised by Gungdilkew's confident words. "I will," she said, "but what makes you so sure?"

Gungdilkew smiled and placed their hand on her shoulder, branch resting gently. "Because you would do anything for Graystone, and because you have a good and strong heart."

Kuin felt her skin redden slightly at the compliment. "You barely know me," she said looking down. "I'm not as good as you think."

Gungdilkew lifted her chin gently. "You protected me, a fairy that you barely knew, and Chis. You stood up to your parents when you didn't have to. Perhaps you are better than you think."

Kuin couldn't stop the small smile that formed on her face.

Glem cleared his throat. "Perhaps you could take us to your home? I would love some tea and, if you have

any, I've read much about the berry loaves that earth
fairies make and would very much like to try one."

As B'nakma watched the pompous Wise lead Kuin into the woods, the magic there blocked his view. He reached out and grabbed the goblet he had been drinking from and threw it at the wall, wine splashing in every direction.

Not what you planned, Graystone's voice asked in his mind.

B'nakma had full control over the shell of Graystone, but somehow the boy's mind refused to let go.

"It matters not," he said out loud, enjoying the use of his physical voice. "Soon I will have the strength that I need to end your sister and her pathetic bloodline for good. The Mothers speak to her, they lead her. But without their Dragon bodies, they are meaningless. I doubt the people of Hilcha will even resist. They are fractured, fighting between themselves. I shall give them the order they seek."

I don't have a sister. What are you talking about?

B'nakma laughed. "Ah, yes. Indeed you do, but I suppose you never knew. She knows now, and it makes her that much more desperate to save you. She will come willingly to her death."

It finally fell into place for Graystone, the last pieces locking together like a puzzle that he didn't even realize he had been building. *Kuin is my sister? How? I realize that this world is different, but I'm pretty sure black is black everywhere, and Kuin is as white as snow.*

B'nakma sighed. He had been ignoring the boy, but with Kuin out of his sight this would serve as a distraction from his anger. "She is your half-sister; you share a father."

My dad cheated on my mom? Graystone tried to reconcile the idea of his parents not having the perfect marriage that he remembered.

"No of course not. Your father was married to your mother. She was a warrior, fierce and strong. She also had a temper, one that broke your father. When he finally took a stand, he left and fell in love with Heekah."

You're lying. My father never left my mother. They died together, in an accident. I was there.

B'nakma squeezed the bridge of his nose. "Silly boy. I forget you really don't know anything. The memories that you have of your parents aren't real. My demons put them in your mind. I wanted them to make you suffer, so they made sure that you had plenty of happy memories before watching your 'parents' die. But none of it was real."

Graystone was silent. A lie? His whole life was a lie? And Kuin was his sister? He loved her as such, but he had never known. *That's why Robert said that I was as important to Hilcha as she was.*

"Yes, that damned cat. I suppose it was convenient that he found the two of you and brought you here, but I would've preferred not to have her reunited with her parents."

Cat, Graystone asked, confused. *Robert is a man.*

"Robert is a cat. His real name is Bo, though your father and his wife have many names for him. He was there the night that we took the two of you from them. He followed you to earth, and it would seem he spent his life searching for you."

What the-

"It doesn't matter," B'nakma interrupted. "In the end none of it matters, because I know Kuin's biggest weakness: you. And when the time comes, she will come for you, and I will let you watch as I kill her slowly, painfully, draining her magic and leaving nothing but a broken husk."

I won't let you.

"You have little choice. I have full control-"

This time it was Graystone that interrupted B'nakma. Not with words, but by making his finger twitch. "I will have full control," he corrected, pinning the errant finger to the table. "By the time I face her, you will be completely mine."

✱✱✱

Glem sat at the table in Gungdilkew's home and wiped the last few crumbs of berry loaf from his mouth with his sleeve. "That was as good as the rumors claim, thank you for allowing me to experience it."

Gungdilkew nodded. "You're very welcome. But may I ask, why are you here?"

"Because I knew that Kuin would like the opportunity to see you and your brother again. And also, because the magic of this place will block B'nakma from being able to see her."

"He can see me," Kuin asked, unsettled.

"Oh, yes, I'm quite sure of that. He can see most of the land and what goes on in it. His demons and shades are everywhere, and they have spent decades hiding and blending in. Through their eyes, I have no doubt he has been watching you."

"And Graystone? Can he see as well?"

Glem shrugged. "That I do not know. If your brother yet lives inside of B'nakma, it is possible. But we have to assume that B'nakma by now has control of your dear Graystone's body, and has likely locked his mind away. If your brother is strong, he may still yet live."

"He does. I know he lives. If he didn't, I would feel it. And if he were dead, then this would all be for nothing."

Glem reached across the table and rested his hand on Kuin's. "Dear child, this is about saving Hilcha. This is about your parent's lives, your life, your new friends' lives," he said gesturing at the fairies. "This is much bigger than your brother."

Kuin shook her head. "Not for me. My purpose is to save my brother now. That is what I care about."

"Perhaps it is. But if that is all that you care about, then you will fail."

"Then I'll fail. I don't want to live my life without him. And I don't want to be in this world, learning and experiencing everything new, without him."

"We shall see," Glem said, before turning to Gungdilkew. "May I ask a favor of you?"

"Ask, yes. Receive, perhaps," they replied.

"I would like for you to take us to your fairy queen."

Gungdilkew snorted. "You want me to take her, the Princess of Hilcha, to the Queen of the Fairies? Why? So that she can lock Kuin up, punish her for the crimes of the other humans?"

Glem smiled. "Your queen would not do that. She is reasonable, and she would not cross a Wise of the Mothers. No matter how much the inhabitants of Hilcha may hate each other right now, the Mothers will always be respected."

Gungdilkew shook their head. "No, I can't do that. It's not safe, and I won't put Kuin in harm's way."

"Kuin is already in harm's way. She has been for
her whole life. If we cannot get all of the species of this
world to unite, then we have already lost. All I ask is that
you take us to the queen. I am certain that Kuin will do the
rest."

"What is 'the rest'? What am I supposed to do or
say that can make up for the horrors that humans have put
the fairies through," Kuin asked, resentment in her voice.

"There is nothing that you can say or do to change
what has already been done. However, the fairies too
have murdered humans. No one has clean hands
anymore. And we must work together to defeat B'nakma.
Standing united is the only hope we have."

Gungdilkew shook their head. "No," they said
again, "I will not do as you ask."

"He's right," Kuin started. But before she could
finish the thought, her eyes went fire red and her body
lifted out of her seat. "The child will unite all of Hilcha.
Start with the fairies. Visit all of the species, let her meet
with the leaders and bring them together. The fate of one,
or the future of all."

18

"Are you freaking crazy," Fyan snapped at Glem when he told them of his plan.

Glem had returned to the house without Kuin, and when they sat in the living room and he told her parents why, they were less than pleased.

"It is the will of the Mothers. And it is the only way."

"And you just left her there with those fairies?"

Glem smiled. "Gungdilkew and Chis are their names, and they are no threat to your daughter."

"Maybe not, but I'm starting to wonder if perhaps you are."

Heekah put a hand on her husband's shoulder. "He is a Wise, and the Mothers know what they are doing. There may be a risk, but it does make sense. We must be united."

"We've lost the children once to B'nakma, I'm not going to just let her wander into danger and risk losing her to some fairy queen. It's bad enough that Graystone is still gone, I won't lose our daughter."

Heekah was going to follow her husband when he stormed out of the house, but Glem held up a hand. "Give him a moment."

Heekah sighed and slumped into a chair. "I can't lose her again, he's right. I trust the Mothers, I do, I know my own is there with them. But how do we let our daughter that we just got back go off into danger?"

Glem smiled reassuringly. "You just said that you trust the Mothers. That is how you let Kuin go to become the princess she was born to be. Faith. The Mothers will protect her, I have no doubt. Harm will not come at the hands of any of Hilcha's people, the only real threat to her is B'nakma. And with a united Hilcha, and the Mothers guiding us, B'nakma will be destroyed once and for all."

Tears formed in Heekah's eyes, but she wiped them away furiously. "I just want her to be a little girl. This is not fair."

"None of this is," Glem agreed. "It's not fair that your child and her brother were taken, it's not fair that Graystone lies in the clutches of B'nakma, and it's not fair that the fate of our world lies in the hands of your daughter. But it does. And I, for one, have the utmost faith in her."

Heekah smiled smally. "Me too."

Glem stood and turned to leave. "If you will give me your leave, Your Highness, I would have a word with your husband before I return to the child."

On the porch, Fyan sat smoking his pipe. "I heard what you two said. My children are not pawns."

Glem shook his head. "No, no they most certainly are not. We are the pawns, I'm afraid. It is our job to guard and protect them, while they go boldly into danger to conquer evil. Your son is already out of our reach, at least for now. Your daughter, the future queen, is the one that we must rally all of the other pawns around. Together, with the might of Hilcha and the Mothers, we may just succeed in protecting our dear princess."

"How," Fyan asked. "How do I let my daughter go off into hostile lands?"

"Just like I told your wife: faith. Have faith."

Fyan scoffed. "Whatever faith I had died when my babies were ripped from our world all those years ago."

Glem smacked Fyan upside the head. "Then find it for your children's sake. Your daughter will need her father there by her side, and your son will want to see his father when he is rescued."

Fyan fought the urge to strike Glem back. He knew that what he said made sense, but the fear for his children was nearly crippling. "It's not like me being there is going to help her. I have no magic. I'm just a man."

"I am also just a man with no magic," Glem said gesturing to himself. "We have been chosen by the Mothers, you as the father of your children, and me as your daughters trainer. We both must fulfill our duties."

Before Fyan could argue anymore, Glem turned. "I will return to your daughter, and we will stay with the siblings this night. Comfort your wife, prepare yourself. Tomorrow we will return, and when we do the journey to the Queen of the Fairies will begin."

"Please, take some dinner with you," Heekah said, coming out onto the porch with a small tuck. "There is enough for you and Kuin, and the fairies if they would like some."

Glem nodded a thank you, and left.

When Glem returned to the home of Gungdilkew, Kuin had Chis on her shoulders and Gungdilkew was chasing them around.

"Wise," Chis called out, "I'm flying on a dragon!"

The joy on all of their faces gave Glem pause. How many more innocent moments like this would they have? Indeed, how many moments like this had Kuin ever truly experienced? Her life had not been one of play and fun, and he couldn't help but feel sad for the time that she lost, and for how quickly she would have to grow up even more.

"What's wrong," Kuin asked, slowing as she passed near to Glem.

The man smiled. "Nothing, my Princess. Enjoy your play, we will talk later. Your mother sent me with some provisions, so we will eat when you are hungry."

Glem made his way into what passed as the kitchen in the home, and Gungdilkew followed. "I'm surprised that her parents allowed her to stay."

Glem shrugged. "I don't think that either of them are pleased with what must occur, but I think they both realize it is for the good of all. And your friend is very stubborn, likely a fight that they did not want to have with her."

They smiled. "She is stubborn, isn't she? I think that will be one of her strongest attributes in what is to come."

"It may very well be," Glem agreed. "Heekah sent me with food, would you care for some?"

Gungdilkew pulled a face. "Human food? No thank you."

"Very well. Do you have a room for us for the night? I would very much like to rest early, we have a long day ahead of us tomorrow."

"Of course, I have rooms for both of you. When do you plan to leave for the queen?"

"At first light," Glem said, pulling a small piece of bread from the tuck and sitting down. "We will go to her parent's home, and then from there begin our journey. If all goes well we shall be in Dispok by nightfall the following day."

Gungdilkew smiled. "It will not take that long."

Glem raised an eyebrow but said nothing.

Kuin and Chis entered the kitchen. "I'm starving," Kuin said. "It's hard work being a dragon."

Chis smiled. "Can I fly more after you eat?"

"She needs to rest," Gungdilkew said, lifting their brother. "And so do you. It will be time to sleep soon. Go make sure Kuin and Glem have everything they need, please."

When Chis scurried off, Gungdilkew sat down at the table. "I'm not sure what kind of reception we will receive in Dispok."

"Dispok," Kuin asked in between bites of the food her mother had sent.

"The fairy capital," Glem answered. "A truly beautiful place, though I've only read of it and seen depictions."

"I can assure you that the depictions do not do it justice," Gungdilkew smiled wistfully before their expression sobered. "But the gates of Dispok have not welcomed humans in nearly twenty years. Even before the princess was taken, relations with humans were icy. There were attempts made to take the lives of members of the Royal Family, and even some claims that there were assassins sent for the Queen herself."

"Yes, I have heard the stories. The rumors that reached me on the island were just that, rumors. In fact, many did not even believe that there were any actual incidents," Glem shrugged, taking another bite of his roll.

"Of course the humans would claim that. My father was there then though, and he himself witnessed one of the would-be assassins being captured."

"Perhaps," Glem acknowledged, "but proof was never provided, and none ever admitted to-"

"And you expect them to admit to attempting to kill the queen," Kuin interjected. "From what I've seen in just my short time here, I'm not surprised, nor do I doubt the voracity of those claims. Humans are animals."

"We are all animals. Nothing more than creatures, any of us. But the world that you have returned to is not the same one that you were taken from," Glem shrugged. "In the end, we will be grateful for the opportunity to meet with the queen, it is the only way forward."

Gungdilkew nodded. "I'm sure that you will be brought before her, but I cannot give you assurances of how you will be treated. She's not likely to harm either of you, she wouldn't want that kind of diplomatic nightmare. But your reception will be cold at best."

Glem finished his bread and wiped his mouth. "We shall deal with that when the time arises. If you'll excuse me," he said, standing from the table, "I will retire for the evening. I suggest that you do the same sooner than later, Your Royal Highness."

Kuin bristled at his use of the title but nodded. "I will."

19

"I hope that you will be comfortable. If you need anything else, please just let me know. Our home is yours tonight."

Kuin looked at Gungdilkew as she sat down on the soft, earthen bed. "I'm sure this will be perfect. Thank you," she said with a smile.

Gungdilkew stopped as they got to the door. "If I may, I do think that you are the best thing that has happened to Hilcha in many years. If anyone can unite us, it will be you."

Kuin smiled softly at her friend. "I don't even know what this world looks like. Other than my family, I've only really met you, Chis, and Glem. I don't know how I can do what is asked of me."

"You will know as you are doing it. The way that you ran to me in the forest when your parents were…well, that is the sign of a queen that is not only strong and wise, but kind and understanding."

Kuin stood and walked to them. "I am not a queen and I never will be," she said, taking their hand in hers. "But what was being done to you, what has been done to your people, is not okay and if I can change it at all I will."

They squeezed her hand. "It's not just my people, it's everyone. The Wise is correct about that much, our people have all done terrible things and we need someone to unite us. But you will be queen one day, even if you don't think that you will. It is your right, your weight to bare."

Kuin let their hand go and turned away, tears forming that she didn't want them to see. "I will not. I am not meant to live that long."

Gungdilkew put their hand on her shoulder. "That is not something that you can know."

"No," she asked whirling around, not caring anymore if they saw her tears. "'The fate of one, or the future of all'? I think that's pretty freaking clear," she all but yelled at them, her voice cracking.

Gungdilkew looked at their friend as she again sat down on the edge of her bed and wiped her eyes. "You do not even know exactly what that means."

"What else could it mean," she asked, a mixture of frustration and pleading in her tone. She wished with all of her heart that there was another explanation, but it seemed clear that it was her life or everyone's.

"I don't know, but until you get to that moment, you don't either. But you're here now, and you have people around you that will protect you and fight beside you when the time comes."

Kuin put her head in her hands and covered her eyes. "I am here now. And I don't know why I'm here."

"Because this is your home," they said, sitting beside her and putting their arm around her shoulder.

"I wish it was," she said, not bothering to hide the tears in her voice. "It was supposed to be. I came here, I brought Graystone here, so that we could have a better life. And now he's in the clutches of some evil god that I didn't know existed a few weeks ago, and I feel more alone than I have ever felt. This doesn't feel like home. Home is a world away."

Gungdilkew stood to leave. "I am sorry that you feel that way. Please just know that there are those here who would give their lives for yours," they said, walking to the door.

Kuin looked up at him with tears running down red cheeks. "Please don't leave. I'm sorry. I know that there are those here that care about me, but I feel so alone and so far from everything I've known for my whole life."

They walked towards her, taking their more human form as they did. Wiping the tears from her cheeks, they held her face in their hands.

"Please stay. I don't want to be alone," Kuin asked when they turned to leave again.

"I will stay until you fall asleep," they said, sitting down in a chair.

"No. Please. I don't want to be alone tonight," Kuin said as she lay down and pulled the covers over herself.

"I...that may not be appropriate princess," Gungdilkew stammered.

Kuin shook her head. "I don't care. I don't want to be alone, and I need a friend."

Gungdilkew climbed into the bed next to her, and she lay her head on their chest. Putting their arm around her, they rubbed her back as she wept.

****

The next morning, Kuin woke up to the sound of knocking. "Just a moment," she said.

She sat up, and realized that Gungdilkew was still sleeping next to her. "Hey, it's morning," she said, shaking them gently.

"Just a few more minutes," they mumbled.

When someone knocked on the door again, Gungdilkew sat straight up. "Oh crap, I didn't leave," they said, looking around.

Kuin smiled as she got out of the bed. "No, I asked you to stay."

Walking over, she opened the door enough to see that it was Glem.

"Good morning, Your Royal Highness," he said, entering the room before she could stop him.

"I was hoping you would be awake by now, we need to return to your-"

He stopped when he saw the tree fairy in her bed.

"Gu…Gungdilkew," he stammered. "I didn't realize that you were in here as well."

"I didn't want to be alone, and I asked him to stay with me."

"Yes, well, Princess, this is highly inappropriate. You are much too young to have a male in your bed, and if anyone found out-"

"First off, Gungdilkew is not a male. Second off, I'm almost fifteen," she said. "And third, he simply stayed with me so that I wasn't alone; and, really, it's not anyone's damn business."

"I'm not entirely sure that your parents would agree. You are the heir to the throne, and this would cause scandal before you even begin to attempt to unite Hilcha."

"My parents won't know, and Gungdilkew is my friend, and I needed a friend."

She glanced at Gungdilkew as she said it, and saw the look on their face. Hurt? Embarrassment? Regret? She wasn't sure.

"He is right. I'm sorry that I let you be put in this position," they mumbled as they stood and nearly ran from the room.

Glem sighed. "Princess, you must think of more than just yourself right now. If word got out that you had spent the night with-"

"Word will not get out," Kuin snapped. "And I am going to do everything I can to save my brother, and if I can help Hilcha along the way, great, but I'm going to put my brother and I first. And I needed someone to be with me last night."

Glem opened his mouth as if to respond, but closed it.

"Good. Then if you are finished lecturing me, go. I will be down when I have dressed for the day."

As Glem left, she realized that her words made her sound very much like a spoiled princess ordering away a servant. But she was not a spoiled princess, and Glem was not her servant. She was just a girl whose home was a world away, a girl that missed her brother, and a girl that needed someone to care about her in the world she found herself in.

Ten minutes later, the group was leaving the fairy's home and heading to the home of her parents.

"When we arrive," Gungdilkew said, not looking at anyone in particular as they walked, "I think it would be best if Chis and I stayed at the edge of the woods."

Kuin groaned. "No. I'm not going to have the two of you, my friends, hiding away because of what people might say."

"Besides," Glem added, "we have to leave the woods to get to Dispok in any case."

"Actually," Gungdilkew said, "there is another, much more efficient, route. If you would just bring Kuin's parents back here, we can save much time by going my way."

Chis came and took her hand. "Please, don't make me leave the woods."

Kuin stopped and kneeled to look Chis in his eyes. The child was scared, his leaves rustling with his small trembling. "I won't."

They walked the last few minutes to the edge of the woods in silence.

20

"They want us to what," Fyan asked incredulously, standing on his front porch with Heekah.

"Gungdilkew has asked that we bring the two of you to the woods. They have another way of getting to Dispok it would seem," Glem repeated the fairy's request.

"I'm not going into those woods when the way to Dispok is not that way. Bring them here."

Kuin ran her hand down her face in exasperation. "I'll tell you what. You," she gestured to her mother and father, "can stay here, or go the way you know, or go on a vacation, I don't care. Glem and I will be following Gungdilkew, and we will go the way they leads us, to *their* city."

In truth, Kuin didn't know how to get to Dispok. She didn't know north from south in this world. She had no idea what the world looked like outside of her parents' home, and the forest where her friends lived. But she trusted Gungdilkew. And since Glem seemed to be okay with following the fairy, she wouldn't hesitate to take a shorter route.

"Look," she said, taking a deep breath. "I want you both to come. I don't want to do all of this without you. But this is how we are going. So, the choice is yours."

She turned and walked back towards the woods.

Heekah put her hand on her husband's arm. "Come on, let's trust our daughter," she said as she slung her tuck over her shoulder and began following Kuin.

Fyan threw his hands up in defeat. "Fine. It's madness to go that way, there is no bridge that crosses the ocean, but sure, let's go that way," he mumbled as he followed.

When they got back to the woods, Chis was holding onto his sibling's leg, peaking out from behind at Fyan and Heekah.

Kuin walked to him and picked him up. "Come on, you don't need to be afraid."

She carried him to her parents. "Mom, dad, this is Chis. Chis," she said, gesturing to her parents, "this is my mom and dad. They won't hurt you; I promise."

Chis whispered something into Kuin's ear that Heekah couldn't hear, but when Kuin smiled and nodded, Chis held out his hand to the older woman. "Kuin said I can show you where we live when we go back by my home."

Gungdilkew bristled at this, but did not object.

"Then lead the way," Heekah said, smiling as the young fairy dragged her forward by the hand.

As Kuin took Chis's other hand and walked with them, Chis chattering on about the woods and this creature or that berry, Fyan fell back to be closer to Gungdilkew.

"Why are we going this way? Do you have a boat?"

The fairy took a moment to answer. "I would ask you to trust me," they said, "but since I know that you don't, I will just tell you what you want to know. No, there is no boat. At the tip of this land, there is an old bridge. You won't find it on any human maps, it has long been unused and seemingly in a state of disrepair."

"Great," Fyan huffed, "an old bridge that isn't safe to cross. That is a long stretch of ocean and a crumbling old bridge is not something I relish the idea of you leading my daughter across."

Gungdilkew stopped, their sibling and the others seemingly not noticing. "You may not believe this, but I care about your daughter. I would not lead her into harm. And, despite the fact you may believe her to be still just a child, she is so much more than that. She is caring, strong, a natural leader, and she has the blood of the Dragons running through her veins. She knows what she is doing by trusting me, so please, just listen to her instead of trying to control her."

Fyan opened his mouth to object, but Gungdilkew did not stop. "What happened to her as a babe is not your fault. But she did not have you or her mother growing up. And as much as you may wish to make up for lost time, she doesn't need you to protect and shield her now. She knows how to handle herself. She needs your support, she needs you and Heekah by her side, step by step, to help her know that she is not alone anymore. But not to tell her what to do. And," they said, walking again, "I said the bridge *seemed* to be in disrepair. It is not."

Gungdilkew thought they heard Fyan mumble something about 'still her father', but they didn't turn back and soon caught up to the rest of their group.

Heekah looked at her husband. He was a stubborn man, she knew, but she also knew that he was a caring man that would do anything for his children and his land. "Settled," she asked softly.

Fyan just nodded and touched her shoulder reassuringly.

As they walked, the group fell into silence. Glem followed them in the rear, Fyan walking at the head of the group with Gungdilkew.

One foot in front of the other, the group plodded towards their destination. After about an hour, Chis got tired and when Gungdilkew paused to pick him up, Heekah stopped him.

"Chis, would you mind if I carried you?"

Chis looked to his older sibling who just nodded.

"Can I pretend that you are a dragon too," Chis asked excitedly as Heekah put him on her shoulders.

"Of course, you will be my brave warrior, riding on the wings of a great dragon," she said with a gleam in her eye.

She looked at her daughter. Obviously at some point Kuin had allowed Chis to pretend on her shoulders. Her heart soared at the thought of it, an image of Chis on Kuin's shoulders, arms spread as if flying. It was such a small thing; but this small thing hadn't happened in so very long. A tree fairy, playing alongside a human child. Their world had been so tense, on the razors edge of all-out war between the species, for so long. It may be a small thing, but in her heart, Heekah knew that it was a glimpse at what was to come; a glimpse at a world where her daughter would unite them all again, and defeat B'nakma once and for all.

The edges of a lake came into view, both ends tipped with dense forest.

"Is there a boat to cross, or will we need to go through the woods," Fyan asked.

"A boat will be provided, if the elders agree. If not, we shall walk through their shade," Gungdilkew said cheerfully.

Fyan was visibly annoyed by the non-answer, but to Kuin's relief he did not argue it.

A short time later, they reached the north tip of the lake, the woods dense and dark from the outside.

"I would go into the woods with just Kuin," Gungdilkew said, turning to face the group.

"I'm sure you would," Fyan snapped, "but I will go where my daughter goes."

"Fyan," Glem said, cutting tension. "Perhaps allow your daughter to decide."

"We will not go far," Gungdilkew added.

Kuin walked up next to her friend and took their hand. "Lead the way."

Fyan watched anxiously as his daughter and the fairy approached the edge of the wood and disappeared inside, the trees seeming to swallow them up.

"I don't like this," he said.

In the forest, Kuin walked for a moment, pleased by the beauty and silence that surrounded her. No, not silence, she realized. Simply the absence of voices or any other sounds from people.

The forest was alive with sound, birds flying, their wings flapping and chirps serenading her as she walked. The brush rustling and vibrating with the sounds of small animals going about their business. Somewhere in the distance an animal grunted, a few seconds later an answering grunt from its mate. Then there were the leaves. The leaves seeming to whisper, almost melodic in their sound. A soft song with words that she couldn't quite make out, as if they were just out of the reach of her mind.

"This is beautiful," she said, turning back to Gungdilkew. But they were not there. In fact, Kuin couldn't even see the path behind her that she had just taken. Turning around again, the path that she was following seemed to have disappeared completely. A moment of panic rose in her chest, when Kuin realized that the sounds of the forest were now drowned out by the sounds of the leaves, their song no longer a quiet melody, but instead coming harsh and broken. The words began forming in her mind as they became even louder, her native language sounding harsh and angry on the wind.

Dag. Leave.

Gbub dfif. Not welcome.

Siw, wingwo u snam. Human, killer of wood.

The forest began to shrink around Kuin. The trees coming closer and closer, until branches began wrapping around her body like vines on a building, enveloping her. Fear coursed through her body as the voices became louder, chanting as one.

Wul iw, ngib fwim fi. Burn her, as humans have us.

She opened her mouth to beg, but thick branches covered her mouth, silencing her. She squeezed her eyes shut as the bark of the branches began nearing her them, her lids closing seconds before they were covered.

She stood in the middle of the forest, as the branches of the trees wrapped her entire body.

Ngwo siw, ilt kmaigu. Kill the human, avenge our dead.

Kuin wanted to scream, she wanted to beg for mercy. Fear gripped every part of her. She could feel her power thrumming at the edges of her reach, summoning her to grasp it and free herself, to destroy this evil that entombed her.

But she couldn't, her fear locked her mind in place the way the limbs of the forest locked her body.

"Release her," she could hear a voice. The tone made it seem as though the voice was screaming, but the sound was muffled, quiet.

"Release her," it said again. "She is here to restore unity to Hilcha. She brings the power of the Dragon to defeat B'nakma for a final time," the voice tried to reason with the forest.

She felt the branches by her eyes ripped away. As she opened them, her sight cleared just in time to see Gungdilkew being lifted up from the forest floor, their limbs being pulled in every direction by the limbs of the trees around them.

Perhaps you should die with the human, the leaves whispered, hissed, in the breeze. *Perhaps you have brought her here to kill the queen, to finish burning your kind!*

Traitor, another voice screamed on the now increasing wind.

More voices came, their sound overlapping, blending, and even through her still covered ears the sound was deafening.

Kill the traitor!

Avenge our brothers!

Tear them both apart and send the pieces back to the other humans!

Kuin watched as Gungdilkew's arms were being ripped from their body, wood creaking before snapping and splintering. She could feel the power still there, but closer and...different. Kuin reached for the power, fear overpowered by the sight of her friend being ripped apart before her eyes.

Heat started building in her core, radiating from her chest to her arms, to her legs, before she felt her entire body burn. It didn't hurt, but the heat was intense. Flames began licking at the limbs holding her, and the voices in the wind howled and screeched.

She felt herself drop free, her body no longer held, burnt wood surrounding her, ash and smoke swirling around her.

"Release them," she said, throwing out her hand and watching as flames burnt the limbs holding Gungdilkew.

The power was intoxicating, and she could feel herself wanting more. She wanted to burn this entire forest to the ground.

Gungdilkew dropped, their eyes locked on Kuin's. But she didn't have eyes. Her body glowed brightly, and where her eyes once were, flames danced.

"No," Gungdilkew cried out as she threw her hands out again, burning trees, grass, shrubs, and any living thing around her.

But she couldn't stop. She needed more. She grabbed at the power, and she felt her heat rise even more. She felt herself begin to lift from the bed of the forest, turning slowly and throwing out flames at everything she saw.

21

Fyan had been saying something to Glem, but what he was talking about was instantly forgotten as the acrid smell of burning wood overpowered them. Then came the smoke. So much smoke; ash and flames licking above the canopy of the forest before them.

"No," Heekah exclaimed, grabbing Fyan's arm when he began to run towards the forest.

Fyan whirled and looked at his wife.

"It needs to be me," Heekah explained. "Whatever is happening in there, it needs to be me. Flame can't hurt me."

Understanding dawned in Fyan's eyes. The dragon. Something had awakened the dragon in his daughter.

Suddenly, Heekah heard Bo's voice in her mind. They hadn't even brought the cat, they hadn't even thought of the cat, when they left the house. But apparently, the ever loyal Bo had followed.

The young one, where is he, Bo asked, whirling in circles franticly.

"Where is young Chis," Glem mirrored the white haired cat's concern, looking around.

"There," Heekah cried, pointing to the edge of the woods.

Chis' small body was running into the burning forest, and after only a second he disappeared into the smoke.

By the time Heekah had found Chis, Bo had made it halfway to him. When the fairy vanished into the smoke, Bo didn't slow but ran in behind him.

Stay there, I'll find her.

Heekah had no intention of listening, and the entire group ran towards the burning forest.

At the edge of the woods, the trees barely visible through dense smoke, the party stopped. The branches of all of the trees had twined themselves together, forming a wall.

"Kuin," Heekah called out.

Soon the voices of Heekah, Fyan, and Glem were all calling out, names barely audible through their coughs, the smoke choking them.

"Kuin!"

"Chis!"

"Bo!"

Over and over they called the names of the other half of their party, until the only sound was that of wood cracking as it burned, and their coughing. They had to get back, walk away to clear air.

Kuin was lost in the power, her mind thinking of nothing but destruction as she watched the forest burn. She made her way deeper in to the woods, launching flames at anything that wasn't burning.

She saw movement off to her right, and she spun, throwing both hands out as a stream of flame raced towards its target.

But when it reached the source of the movement that had caught her eye, it wrapped around the object.

Anger flared in Kuin. This forest would bend to her will, nothing would be left. She reached deeper, brought more heat. The flames still encircled her target, whatever was inside, protected in a sphere of magic.

Princess, stop, a voice said in her mind, and she pointed one hand in the direction of something small and white.

Too late Kuin realized that the voice and it's source was her cat. The cat that had come to another world, had followed her and her brother to another world to protect them.

"Bo," she cried out.

She stopped the flames in his direction, but he was already burned, his white fur turned to a mess of burnt skin. The protection that he had been casting fell, and Kuin saw what he had encircled with his magic. Or, rather whom.

Her scream was full of pure pain as the small, burned pile of sticks that had once been Chis smoldered.

Kuin ran to the little fairy, and was shocked to see his eyes open.

"P...pr...princess," the fairy sputtered and coughed.

"Don't speak," Kuin said, scooping up his burned limbs and pulling him to her.

"Oh Chis," she said, tears flowing down her cheeks, "I'm so sorry. I'm so, so sorry."

The sound of anguish came from behind her, as Gungdilkew's burned and smoking form stumbled close enough to be visible.

"No," they screamed and dropped down beside her. "How could you?"

Gungdilkew tore Chis from Kuin's arms, and Kuin stood, backing away.

"I'm sorry," she said again. "I'm sorry. I'm sorry."

She walked backwards, unable to take her eyes off of the young fairy in Gungdilkew's arms. Her foot caught on something, and she fell back. Looking toward her feet, two eyes, one blue and one golden, looked back at her. Bo was burned, his toe beans raw and reddened by the burns. His breaths came in gasps.

You can fix this.

Kuin shook her head. No, there was no fixing this. She had lost control. She looked around the forest in shock. Everything was either on fire, or still smoldering. She did this. How many had she killed in this forest? How many fairies were in the trees that she burned? How many animals had she killed, or destroyed their homes?

What did I do?

You made a mistake, Bo's deep voice purred in her mind, no trace of his pain in the words. *But the mistake was not yours alone. We did not prepare you.*

An ache formed in her heart, and Kuin squeezed her eyes closed. She tried to block out the crackling of wood burning, the acrid smell of smoldering vegetation, but she couldn't. *What did I do?*

A new voice, female and strong, came into her mind. *You awakened. We sent you Glem, but he did not prepare you in time. There is much blame to be passed around. But,* the voice said soothingly, *now is not the time for blame.*

"Who are you," Kuin said, this time out loud.

I am Gwimsum. I am your mother's mother.

"How do I fix this," Kuin asked beggingly.

I will show you; reach for your power once more. Do so with love. Do so with empathy. Do so with the desire to heal.

The thought of using her powers again made Kuin wretch. Bile stung her throat as the voice of her grandmother once again spoke to her mind.

Do it now. Reach for your power, do so with all of the love that you have in your heart for those whom you have harmed today, and do not let go. Allow yourself to be lost in it, go deeper than you did when you burned the world.

Kuin felt heat rise again inside of her, but a different kind of heat. Instead of flame and fire, burning orange and red, she felt white heat. Bright, white hot heat pulsed deep in her core, and she reached for it.

✱✱✱

Heekah felt the power surging from her daughter on the other side of the wall. The smoke cleared and a pillar of white flame shot towards the heavens from the forest in front of her.

Go to her.

Heekah hadn't heard her mother's voice in years; she had begun to wonder if the Mothers were even still alive, still watching over them. The emotion at hearing her own mother's voice once again flared for only a second before she obeyed the command, pushing down the love and relief that Gwimsum's words brought to her.

The smoke had been blown away, like a small candle being extinguished on a year day cake, by the time she made it back to the wall of limbs that barred their way. Fyan and Glem were behind her in an instant as she reached for her own powers. Dull from years of disuse, when her daughter fully awakened she felt them thrum to life once again. Now, reaching for them, she smiled as red flame flew from her hands and the wall blocking their way splintered.

"Arpi," her husband said quietly.

Heekah turned to her husband, her body glowing, her eyes white flames. "They have awakened."

Fyan started to ask who, but Heekah ran towards the center of the woods as the sounds of giant wings flapped above him.

"The Mothers," Glem said in awe, looking up to see the beautiful scales of a white and golden dragon flying low and fast overhead.

22

B'nakma had been sitting in his bed chambers when he felt the power flood into him. He had been barely able to hold Graystone's mind back from taking over the body that he now owned; his power was weak, and it took all of his strength, leaving nothing extra to rebuild his army.

Graystone had felt it too, felt as what little strength he still had disappeared. *No, you can't have me.*

B'nakma laughed, true joy clear in his laugh. Nothing could stop him from taking Hilcha now. He had known that one day the princess would return, that she would free the Dragons from their prison, and he also had known that with their release he too would be free to return to strength. This was why he had left the children alive all those years ago; the princess for her power, and her brother to use as a vessel.

"You have no more choice here," he smiled as he spoke.

B'nakma pushed Graystone's consciousness down. "I will not extinguish your light completely. Watch," he said, closing the walls of his mind around the boy, "as I destroy your sister, your father, your entire kingdom. Watch as I rebuild this world in my image."

Graystone tried to speak, he tried to push back, to control some part of his body. But the body he once owned was no longer his. He could only watch as B'nakma walked to a looking glass on the wall and admired himself.

Graystone watched in horror as from B'nakma's back, from *his* back, wings unfurled. Not the dark, sinewy things that he had seen when he first arrived, but smooth, scale covered wings.

B'nakma extended his wings to full size, the black scales glistening with a hint of red in the light of the small fire burning in the room's fireplace. A snap of his fingers flared the fire bright and large.

Graystone screamed and beat on the walls of his mind with his fists, but it did nothing. He was trapped. He could only watch and listen as B'nakma smiled into the looking glass.

"Now, we rebuild."

23

Kuin watched in awe as the white flames that she now commanded restored the forest. She had healed Chis and Bo first, tears streaming down her cheeks as their small bodies began returning to their former appearance. Chis, green again, lush and healthy; Bo, white fur again covering his body, toe beans pink instead of burned and blistered.

Kuin had begun turning her healing flame towards the forest, but after a small section of trees, she felt herself begin to weaken. But she dug deeper and pushed herself. Moments later, she felt the world begin to spin.

Rest, your mother and I will finish the healing. Kuin could have sworn she heard he sound of giant wings flapping slow and rhythmic, before her world went black.

Heekah saw her daughter in an unconscious heap, still glowing with her healing flame. The forest around her was scarred and smoldering, save a small patch near her. Bo, Chis, and Gungdilkew huddled around her, Chis shaking her arm crying and begging her to wake up.

As Heekah and the two men behind her ran to her daughter, the woman rested her hand on Gungdilkew's shoulder. With Heekah's touch, their limbs were restored, and their foliage was once again bright and healthy. They all looked to the sky.

Above them Gwimsum soared low. White and golden scales glistened in the sun, light filtering through the bare, burned branches that once formed a green canopy.

Kuin's friends stepped back and kneeled to the Mother Dragon as Gwimsum landed . In each of their minds, Gwimsum spoke. *Rise, come be with your friend.*

As the three returned to Kuin, Gwimsum enveloped the group in her wings. Her white scales began glowing, their brightness even more intensified by its reflection off of her golden scales.

Kuin's mother and father, with Glem beside them covered their eyes. Heekah wept loudly, every emotion of having not only her daughter returned, but also her mother and her full strength, pouring from her in loud sobs. Fyan wrapped his arms around her and held her.

24

Kuin awoke surrounded by her friends and family. The forest around her green and lush, all signs of her rampage completely removed. As her eyes adjusted, she saw the source of the flapping wings that she had heard before she lost consciousness. A beautiful white dragon curled on the forest bed watching her.

Sem, pub u ho pub. Hello, blood of my blood.

Kuin stared in awe. *You are my grandmother?*

The dragon shook gently with what Kuin thought was a laugh, the smile clear in her mind's response. *Once, yes, I was a woman known as Gwimsum. I was mother to your mother. Now I am the Mother of Mothers, the queen of the Dragons.*

I'm sorry.

Gwimsum knew that the child was apologizing for losing control, but she asked why just the same.

I couldn't stop. I hurt my friends. Who knows how many creatures I killed.

Gwimsum looked at her. A child, born to be a dragon, ripped from her world, from her magic, from her family. *Come, sit by me.*

Kuin stood and walked to the dragon, sitting next to her. Gwimsum stretched her wing and gently pulled her granddaughter to her. Kuin did not resist. She rested her head on the beast's side, and as she felt the rise and fall of Gwimsum's chest, heard the gentle 'thum-thum' of her heart, Kuin felt at home in this world for the first time.

When my powers awakened, I was just four years old. My mother, Ksul, had taken away a treat from me. I had snuck into our kitchen and grabbed a sweet roll, hiding in the corner and eating it. My mother found me and took the confection from me. I screamed at her, a brat throwing a tantrum. But my scream burned my throat as I released it. I burned down our home, and my mother barely survived.

Kuin nestled in to her side, and Gwimsum placed her wing over her gently like a soft blanket. *What happened to you?*

Gwimsum let out a small sigh, smoke wisping from her nostrils. *My aunt had felt my awakening and come. She healed my mother, but did not restore our home. Along with my mother, they trained me. Taught me how to control my power, how to use not only my ability to destroy, but also my healing flames. I made other mistakes, lost my temper, burned a boy or two. But I never truly hurt anyone again.*

Kuin smiled at the thought that she wasn't the first to make a mistake, and likely not the last. Her smile faded when she thought of Chis's small body, burnt and smoldering, in Gungdilkew's arms. *How can I ever make right the pain I caused today?*

The dragon turned her head slightly, her eye focusing on Kuin. *I don't think that your friends hold any grudge, in fact, they were quick to come to your side when you fell. If forgiveness is what you seek, then I believe you already have it. But,* Gwimsum paused as if deciding how best to word her next statement, *if you seek to repay them more, then become the unifier that you can be. Be the queen that leads this land to peace, unity, and freedom from B'nakma.*

As if on cue, the restored trees began rustling, their leaves once again bringing melodic words, all of the voices in one chorus.

Brip Kuin, kya'ne u iw ngew nup u ta nup u the kmawok. Hail Kuin, first of her name, healer of worlds and mender of the broken.

Kuin stood at the sound, and all of the trees appeared to bow. She looked around and saw her friends, her parents, with their heads bowed and knees bent. She turned back and saw that her grandmother, Gwimsum, the Mother of Mothers, also bowed low, her head down and wings spread in honor.

****

B'nakma roared with anger. He had watched as the child lost control, reveled as she burned the woods along with any hope of unifying the races of Hilcha. But then, she stopped herself. She had found control, she awakened and tried to right her wrong. She couldn't of course, she was untrained, and her powers were only just coming to her.

But then the wretched Gwimsum was freed when her granddaughter awakened. The same as his prison was broken, and his powers returned, so had the power of the Mother of Mothers. She was once again able to take flight, and likely all that was left of her army of Mothers after their last battle were once again restored.

Balance. He had hoped that he alone would have his power returned to him. But of course, fate had desired balance. And so, he would again build his own army. He would again create more dark creatures, bring forth more demons, trap more souls. When he had rebuilt his army, with his legions at his side, he would destroy the dragons once and for all.

But, before that, he wanted to give Kuin, first of her name, a taste of what was to come.

25

The trees around Kuin's group all parted, and a path lead through the forest, soft and easy to travel. Gwimsum flew back to the Isle of Mothers, promising her granddaughter that she would return when the time was right.

The light filtering through the canopy was turning deep orange and fading.

"Is it much further," Kuin asked, turning to Gungdilkew.

Kuin was still having a hard time accepting that she had been forgiven for her act. She knew that they had all given her their allegiance in the forest. She knew that everyone in the group was either family or friend, save Glem who would go with her regardless because it was the Mothers will. But allegiance isn't the same as forgiveness. And, when she thought about it, did she really want their allegiance? This world was not her priority; saving Graystone was. But she had come to care for at least two of the inhabitants of this world, and when she thought about what she had done to sweet Chis, she knew that she would do anything to earn his forgiveness, even if he had already given it.

"No, in fact," Gungdilkew gestured at the trees ahead of them, "the forest ends."

They were right of course. A moment later, the trees ended and before them was the edge of a cliff. Extending from the edge was a crumbling bridge.

Fyan grunted from the back of the group, making his way up to Gungdilkew and his daughter. "You want us to cross this?"

Gungdilkew smiled. "If you want to get to Dispok, yes."

Glem appeared beside them. "Perhaps we should go back. We've lost a day on this journey, but it may be better to take the traditional route instead."

"Do as you wish. I will cross with Chis. And hopefully," Gungdilkew said, gesturing towards Kuin, "the princess will as well."

Kuin smiled and took their hand. "Yes."

Fyan and Glem both began to protest, but Kuin held up her hand. "If I am to unify Hilcha, I will need to trust those around me. And I trust Gungdilkew. You all bowed before me in the woods. If you truly meant that gesture, then follow me now. If you didn't, feel free to turn back, but do not bother meeting us in Dispok."

Heekah stepped forward. "Lead, daughter."

Kuin looked at her father and Glem. They both gave curt nods, and she turned and walked with Gungdilkew to the edge of the bridge.

"The bridge appears to be in disrepair. However, if you follow us, we will easily cross," the fairy said, taking a step onto the bridge.

With Kuin by their side, Gungdilkew led them. Sections of the bridge had crumbled to time, exposing the rushing water far below. Abandoned carts littered the bridge here and there. But there was a solid path, well maintained and easy to follow. The group was halfway across when a figure appeared from behind one of the old carts, the bright setting sun behind the figure making them difficult to see.

"Where are you going," a man's voice asked.

"To Dispok. Would you join us," Gungdilkew asked, clearly startled by the figure's appearance.

"No, I would not be welcome there."

Kuin recognized the voice now. "Graystone."

"Hello sister," he said, still framed by the bright setting sun.

"Graystone," Fyan asked, his voice breaking.

"Father," he said, holding out his hand.

Fyan ran, faster than he had ever run before, towards his son.

"Fyan, wait," Heekah called out. But it was too late.

Smoke spread behind B'nakma, and large wings unfurled from his back.

"No, please, come," he said, his voice changing, dark and harsh.

Fyan froze in his tracks, twenty feet separating him from the god who was once his son.

Glem walked to Fyan's side. "Go back to your mountain, B'nakma. The Mother's have awakened. Harm any of us, and they will crush you before you see another day."

B'nakma chuckled. "I am aware that they have awakened. I, too, have awakened. And I'd be willing to guess that the princess has as well. I cannot yet defeat you, princess," he said, turning to face Kuin. "But, before we meet again, please, allow me to show you a sample of my power."

The smoke behind B'nakma roiled and swept out, a tornado forming that picked up Fyan.

"Dear old dad," B'nakma said, smiling as the man swirled in the smoke. "How unfortunate for you that you never got to see your son again before you died."

Heekah and Kuin screamed in unison as the tornado spit Fyan out, smashing him into Glem and throwing both of them over the edge of the bridge.

"Until next time, sister," B'nakma said, wings flapping as he took flight. "And next time, you can join your father."

Kuin felt her power begin to heat in her core, but before she could reach for it, B'nakma was gone. Her body went rigid and she spoke in her ethereal voice.

"The boy is gone, now merely a suit worn by a god. His father too is gone. The princess must unite the lands against B'nakma to save Hilcha. The fate of one, or the future of all."

✶✶✶

Kuin recovered from her prophecy and saw her mother standing at the edge of the bridge, Bo by her side, her arms wrapped around herself weeping. Gungdilkew and Chis stood a few feet behind her, Chis's face buried in his sibling's shoulder.

Kuin walked to her mother. It was a strange feeling, watching her father be thrown from the bridge at the hands of someone that looked like her brother. She knew there was no possible way that Fyan could have survived, he and Glem surely had drowned if they were not killed by the impact of the fall. Yet, she didn't feel like her father was dead. She didn't believe that he was gone.

"Mom," she said, putting a hand on the older woman's shoulder. "We have to keep moving."

When her mother didn't respond, didn't even acknowledge her, Kuin repeated herself.

"Why," her mother snapped, whirling on her. "Why should we keep going? B'nakma has his strength, and your father is…".

When her mother's voice trailed off, Kuin wrapped her arms around her and held her as she sobbed.

"He's gone, he's gone," Heekah repeated over and over between sobs.

"I know, but we are not; and we must go forward. We need to get off of this bridge before nightfall."

In truth, nightfall was mere minutes away. The last remnants of light fading.

"Gungdilkew, please lead us," Kuin said, leading her mother away from the edge and following as the fairy did as asked.

Your father would be proud, Bo said to Kuin.

Kuin didn't know for sure if her mother could hear the cat, but she had forgotten that he was even there until he spoke and her mother showed no signs of hearing him.

He was proud I'm sure, the cat said again.

Kuin didn't look at him, and he took a paw and smacked at the jewel hanging from his collar. *Is this damn thing working?*

Kuin let a small smile prick at the edges of her lips. *Yes, it's working.*

There was no further talk, and fifteen minutes later they were across the bridge and in a small patch of trees. Kuin realized that they had no supplies, this trip was supposed to take less than a day and there was no need to expect to shelter for the night. They planned to be in Dispok by now. All of them.

At that thought, tears welled in her eyes, but she did not let them fall. She focused on the now.

"We have no shelter," she said to no one in particular. "But I don't think we can continue tonight. We all need rest."

Gungdilkew smiled, setting down Chis. "Perhaps we will have shelter," they said.

Kuin watched as the fairy closed their eyes and pushed their fingers into the dirt. The trees answered, branches forming above them, around them. Soon, a small hut surrounded them. Small beds, with blankets of moss, lined the forest floor. Walls made of tightly woven leaves sheltered them from the outside world.

The home was like the one that Gungdilkew lived in, though much smaller and not as equipped. But it would meet all of their needs for tonight.

"Thank you," Heekah said, lying down on one of the beds and pulling the blanket up to her.

Gungdilkew simply nodded and gave her a soft smile, before settling in Chis. Soon, the small hut was silent, Bo curled at Kuin's feet. She wasn't sleeping, and she doubted much of anyone else was either.

26

Graystone screamed and flailed, banging his mind on the walls of the prison that B'nakma had locked him in. The small satisfaction that he had once held onto of being able to make the God who controlled his body twitch was gone. He was completely powerless. He watched as his father, a man that he never knew, was thrown over the bridge. Watched as Kuin and her mother had screamed as they watched he and the other man fly over the edge and into the darkness below.

He had wept, cried in a way that he couldn't remember ever crying before; not for his father, though perhaps some part of him mourned the stranger, but for his best friend, for his sister. She had to have known that he wasn't in control, that no part of him had been involved in their father's death. But that only created more tears. Would Kuin believe that he too was dead, destroyed by the darkness named B'nakma?

He felt helpless, trapped in his prison. After what felt like an eternity of crying and screaming, punching and kicking at the walls of his mind, he resorted to begging. Begging B'nakma to speak to him, to let him speak to his sister, to release him and choose another host. The complete silence that he got in return only deepened his desperation, until finally he gave up and too fell silent.

27

Kuin awoke with a start. Her entire group was surrounded and somehow all bound at the wrists and ankles. She counted six fairies around them, all with sharpened spears pointed in their direction. With her mind still groggy from the sleep she hadn't thought she would get, she tried to work out how they could all have been bound without waking.

"Princess," a soft but strong voice said. "You are awake."

Kuin looked at the source of the voice. A tree fairy, not much taller than Gungdilkew, but much more dense, sitting not far from her. Relaxed and smiling at her, and the creature caused her to have an involuntary shiver.

"Who are you, and why are we bound," she asked, twisting at the vines around her wrists.

"I am Kamanghi, the leader of the Queen's Royal Guard."

It took Kuin a moment longer than she would have liked to realize that the fairy was not referring to Queen Briyul, but to the queen of the fairies.

"And why are we bound?"

"The queen wishes to see you. You will be brought before her. However, after you burned Tos, we thought it best to make sure you would not be able to harm us or the queen."

"Who is Tos," Kuin asked, still trying to twist free from her bindings.

Kamanghi laughed mirthlessly. "Are you really so ignorant?"

When Kuin simply stared at the fairy, they continued. "Very well. Tos is the forest that you laid waste to in your anger. The ancient trees there have survived longer than even the Mothers of your kind, and you burned them without thought."

"They attacked Gungdilkew and I, and I defended us." Even as she said the words, Kuin knew they were hollow. What she had done had gone far beyond defending them.

"You trespassed, you burned without discretion, maiming even your own party, your so-called friends. You were not attacked, you were tested; and you failed. Miserably."

Kuin shook her head, but did not argue further. "What is to happen to us?"

Kamanghi stood, and the other fairies snapped to attention. "That is up to the queen. Bring them."

As the other fairies quite effortlessly lifted her group to its feet, Kuin reached for her power. She would control herself; she would not allow herself to succumb to the intoxicating feel of it. But, as she reached for her heat, nothing happened. A moment later, heat did come. But it would not release, it stayed burning in her, pain gripping her and causing her to drop to her knees in a cry.

"Ah, yes, I seem to have forgotten to mention: the bindings around your wrist are from a time before any written history. We cannot replicate the magic in them. But they will prevent you from burning anyone other than yourself. So, I would recommend that you not attempt to use your powers."

Fear gripped Kuin, her newfound powers neutralized. She could do nothing but march beside her captors, her group now smaller than before by her side. Except for the cat; Bo was nowhere to be seen.

✶✶✶

Two short hours later, Kuin was thrown roughly into a dungeon cell. Before the group had entered the woods surrounding Dispok, sacks were put over their heads. She had been looking forward to seeing the capital of the fairy kingdom. Instead, when her hood was removed, the only thing she saw was a barely lit dungeon. As the door to her cell was closed behind her, not iron, but rather thick timber, she crumbled to a heap in the corner of her cell.

Her wrists were still bound, there was barely any light, the smell of decayed earth nearly made her wretch, and unsure where her mother and friends were, she wept.

28

Kuin had lost track of time when the guards finally opened her cell door again. Twice they had slid food through a small gap at the bottom of her cell door, but she had no idea what time or even what day it was.

"On your feet, human," one of the two guards said.

Both were tall and imposing, their limbs thick and covered in scarred bark.

Kuin tried to stand, but she was weak. She hadn't eaten any of the food that had been brought, and she was fairly certain that she hadn't slept for more than a few moments.

The second guard grabbed her and lifted her by her bound wrists. "Up. You are to be judged."

Kuin stumbled along as they dragged her out of the dungeon and into the blinding light of day. By the time her eyes had adjusted, she stood in the center of an arena, stands of fairies surrounding her.

In front of her, her mother, Gungdilkew, and even Chis, were bound and gagged, standing still but looking intently at her.

"You would bind a child," Kuin shouted, not taking her eyes from her group.

The crowd around them gasped audibly. A sharp blow to the back of her knee caused Kuin to drop into a bow.

"You dare speak, before I grant you permission, human," the voice of a woman boomed. Her voice was powerful, but it held almost an amused tone, as if Kuin were nothing more than entertainment. "Have you no respect?"

Kuin turned her fiery gaze to find the source of the voice. She may be unable to use her powers, but she hadn't lost her boldness. "Where I come from, respect is earned. And binding a child is not respectable," she said, standing from the bow.

"Ah, yes, the princess who was stolen," the voice said, "Well, this is not where you come from, or rather, where you were raised. This is Hilcha. And the humans lack of respect is why we are here."

"We are here," Kuin said, half-heartedly twisting her bindings, "because you captured us and had us dragged here."

"Is that so? Were you not on your way here already? Were you not being brought here, shown the way here, by the traitor that stands bound next to your mother?"

Kuin looked to Gungdilkew. Their expression was emotionless, eyes locked with hers. "Traitor," Kuin asked, her eyes not leaving Gungdilkew's. "They simply wanted unity, they wanted to see us work together against B'nakma."

"Noble though their intentions may have been, every living fairy knows that to bring another species, most of all a human, to this land is forbidden. To do so is traitorous, and punishable in only one way."

Kuin's mouth went dry. She knew that the voice meant death. "So, you would punish someone for desiring to stop the bloodshed in this world? Punish them for wanting to have a fighting chance against the God B'nakma?"

"No, I would punish them for breaking our laws. Plain and simple."

"And how will following those laws help you when B'nakma has his full powers? How will killing us help Hilcha?"

There was a pause, the voice seemingly considering this question. "Would you have us throw away our laws? Have us turn our back on our tradition?"

"I would have you think about the next step. We die, your law, your thirst for so-called justice is satisfied, and then what?"

"Then, perhaps, the humans stop killing our kind with impunity. Then, perhaps, the humans see that we will not be cowed."

Kuin scoffed. "Fantastic! You will kill us; the humans, somehow in your perfect scenario, do not retaliate and kill even more of the fairies, and B'nakma comes and kills or enslaves you all. That sounds like a brilliant plan."

A sound, like a large bumble bee, buzzed past Kuin's ear, and a small creature stopped in front of her, hovering a few feet away at eye level. It was a fairy. In fact, it was exactly what she had thought of when she had thought of a 'fairy' before coming here. Beautiful, glowing with magic, and no larger than her thumb, the fairy looked her in the eyes.

"And you think to have a better plan than I, Queen Feni, eighth of my name, ruler of Dispok, capturer of the dragon princess and her mother?"

Kuin looked to her mother. 'The dragon princess'. What a strange thing to hear. She had been being called princess, had been being taught about the world she should have grown up in, had even met her grandmother. But knowing that she had the blood of the dragon in her veins stole away any doubt she may have had. She straightened.

"I do."

The queen laughed. "Then you are as foolish as all humans before you."

The fairy queen flew to the three others from Kuin's group, and hovered before them. "You are all found guilty of conspiring against Dispok. You will have no last words."

The queen turned her back to the three and looked at Kuin. "Commence the hangings," her voice boomed.

A large tree shot up from the earth, thick and lush. As it grew from nothing, the shade allowed Kuin to see her mother and her friends more clearly. Tears were in their eyes, but they showed no other signs of emotion.

Kuin's own eyes burned with tears, and she felt her power begin to heat. "Do not do this, queen. We came to this place as friends, in hopes of a conversation."

Queen Feni flew close to Kuin, merely inches from her. "You came to this place as prisoners. But I am not without mercy. Choose one," she said, gesturing to the trio, "to pay for the transgressions of all of you, and I will allow the rest of you to leave. None else will be harmed unless you return to this place."

An impossible choice. Anger and fear flashed through Kuin, causing her power to heat more. The very thought of unleashing it caused pain to ripple through her, and she lost her balance.

"Now, now, you already know you will only hurt yourself if you try to use your powers. Choose, or I shall choose for you."

Kuin looked at her mother, Gungdilkew, and Chis. How could she choose? Her mother, whom she had been robbed of the opportunity to know. Gungdilkew, the friend with whom she shared a budding yet deep connection, who had comforted her when she needed it. Or Chis, just a child.

Kuin shook her head. "No, I beg you again, do not do this Queen Feni."

The heat rose even more in her. She hated begging this fairy, this cruel queen, but without her powers she had little recourse.

Queen Feni flew high, and her voice boomed to all present. "The human cannot choose one to take the punishment, so I will."

The fairy thrust out her arms, and a vine shot down from the tree, wrapping itself around Chis's small neck. Four more vines shot out, one around each of his wrists, and one around each of his ankles, and began pulling him apart. Chis showed no outward sign of the pain that he must be in, his small body creaking as it was stretched.

Tears welled in Kuin's eyes as she felt the power in her, pulsing and thrumming, begging to be released. She tried to use it, but the pain caused her to drop to her knees, crying out.

At the same time, Chis screamed in agony, the first glimpse that he had given to the pain of his torture.

"Stop," Kuin screamed out.

"I gave you the opportunity to choose. Had you chosen, perhaps young Chis would have been spared."

Kuin was sweating now, not from the scene before her, but from the heat rising in her. She could not act. She had taken action in the woods when her parents had tortured Gungdilkew, and that time she didn't have her powers. But now she did, if only she could access them.

The queen buzzed right in front of her, locking eyes. "They said that they wanted you to unify this land, they said that they thought under your leadership Hilcha could again exist in peace. They said that you would lead Hilcha against B'nakma."

The fairy queen looked at Chis, slowly being stretched, wood still separating and splintering, and then looked back to Kuin and smiled. "You can't even save your friend, impotent human."

Kuin had heard enough. Queen Feni was wrong, she wasn't impotent. She may not be able to save her friend, but she was not impotent.

Kuin reached for her power. It burned, but instead of stopping, she dug deeper, reached farther. Pain gripped her, and she collapsed. Still, she only went deeper. She didn't believe in heaven and hell, but she was certain that this is what hell must feel like if it were real. Her entire body felt as though it was being burned in a pit of fire.

The crowd gasped as Kuin screamed and burst into flame. Her entire body wrapped in bright fire, her bindings on her wrists igniting and turning to ash. Kuin's scream stopped.

It no longer hurt, the pain was gone; her body was engulfed in bright, red flames. The crowd gasped, and Kuin turned to where her friends were and shot a burst of heat towards Chis. But she controlled it like a whip, snapping the vines that held him, but never touching the fairy. Another snap of her flames and the vines holding Heekah and Gungdilkew turned to ash.

Kuin whirled and faced the fairy queen again. "Impotent," she asked. But it wasn't her voice. The voice was a deep, powerful growl. "I will show you impotent."

Kuin reached for every drop of power in her and struck out, Queen Feni flying backwards, engulfed in angry flame. But she didn't burn. The fire went around her, as if she were protected by a bubble.

The queen's guards came towards Kuin and she quickly dispatched them, heat launching them backwards through the air, before they crumbled unconscious to the ground.

"Enough," Queen Feni bellowed, her voice as strong as Kuin's.

Kuin paused. The fairy flew right before her eyes again. "Take your friends and leave."

Kuin looked to where her mother kneeled, holding a crying Chis. Anger flared. "No."

She launched flame again at the queen. The bubble around her held as the force of the heat continued to push her back, Kuin following and not relenting. Slowly, the bubble around Queen Feni failed, first in one spot, then small holes began showing everywhere. The queen cried out as flames singed her hair and wings. Kuin still did not relent, the flames coming from her without pause, the bubble around the queen failing more and more.

Stop. She does not deserve to die this way.

At the sound of Bo's voice in her head, Kuin let the flames return to her. She couldn't see the cat, but she knew he must be near.

She was killing Chis, Kuin protested.

Chis is fine now. Do not make him watch as you burn his queen. Has he not seen enough after what happened in the woods? Should you be killed for the pain you caused him? Or Gungdilkew? Or, me?

Guilt wracked Kuin. She let go of the power that she held to, and her body returned to its normal state. Queen Feni lay in the dirt, her wing burned too badly for her to fly.

Guards had formed a circle around the two of them now, the unconscious guards being dragged off and replaced. Bows were drawn as Kuin walked towards the queen. Kuin waved her hands and the arrows burned, the guards dropping their bows.

Kuin scooped Queen Feni gently into her palms. "I could crush you. I could crush your entire kingdom. But that is not what I want, it is not why I came here today. I will take my mother and our friends and leave if that is your wish. But know this, when B'nakma returns in full strength, aid will not come from myself or any humans. If you think that my fire was bad, the darkness that B'nakma brings is more terrible than anything you could ever imagine."

Light wrapped Kuin's hands as she cupped the Queen. "I seek to unite the whole of Hilcha," she said, standing and looking at the crowd. "Speak of what you saw here today. Speak to others, spread word, of the power and strength of Kuin, first of my name. Speak of how I will not allow those who are my friends to be harmed by anyone."

Kuin looked at her hands, and thrust them up, the queen flying out. "And speak of my mercy. I am powerful but understanding. I will abide no one hurting my friends again. I have shown mercy to your Queen in the hope that we can still be united. But the next person to harm one of my friends will have no mercy, will find no quarter. They will burn with the fires of the Dragon's blood that runs through my veins."

Pride burned bright in Heekah's eyes as she watched Queen Feni land on the ground before her daughter.

"All hail Kuin, first of her name," the fairy queen said, dropping to one knee, "the uniter of Hilcha, the bringer of fire light to banish the darkness!"

29

When Queen Feni had told Kuin that they would feast tonight in her honor, Kuin wasn't sure what she expected. In fact, she wasn't sure what she had even expected Dispok to look like. But this was not it.

The castle was massive, built from living trees. Trees of all heights created tall walls, looming spires topped with vine covered parapets. It was one of the most beautiful sights that Kuin had ever seen.

"Do you like it," Gungdilkew had asked as they approached.

Kuin had been speechless, but nodded and smiled.

Now she sat at tables of dark polished wood. Everything was crafted from the land, there was no metal to be seen. A great feast lay before her, Queen Feni at the center of the long table overlooking the dining hall; Kuin was seated to her right, and to the right of Kuin sat Gungdilkew and Chis. Heekah sat to the left of Queen Feni, and to her left sat what Kuin assumes were important fairies, though she does not know anyone here.

Queen Feni flew gracefully up from her small seat. "Good fairies of Dispok, welcome to this historic evening. We have the honor of having with us the first humans to grace our halls in nearly three decades, Queen Heekah and her daughter, Princess Kuin, first of her name."

The crowd clapped, but the sound was unlike anything that Kuin would expect applause to sound like. Instead of the sound of flesh on flesh, it is a great clatter of wooden hands, a cacophony like bare tree limbs in a harsh storm. When the applause died down, the queen spoke again.

"For years we have watched as the land of men became more crafty, harder to trust. For the past fourteen years, we have hidden here under the oppressive rule of Queen Briyul, watched our mothers, fathers, children and grand children cut down by the blades of man, simply for existing. We have all come to fear and hate the humans. But," the queen landed on the table before Kuin, "a new day has come to Hilcha, even as B'nakma's darkness threatens it."

Kuin smiled softly and bowed her head, as the Queen looked directly at her. "My spies are everywhere, Princess, and I have watched you since the day you returned; since the day that you stumbled, by the luck of the gods, into the home you were meant to have lived in. I watched as you found your friends, Gungdilkew and Chis, in the woods and were kind to them. Watched as your father tortured your friend, and you stepped in and put a stop to it. I watched as you entered Tos, and burned it to ash, burning your friends with it."

Kuin lowered her head, not wanting the tears that welled in her eyes to be seen. The shame at the pain she caused her friends would weigh on her forever.

The Queen went on. "But I watched, as you stopped yourself, stopped a power that you didn't even know you had, let alone were ever trained on how to use. I watched as your grandmother, the great Gwimsum, flew from the Isle of the Mothers for the first time in decades and showed you how to heal those very friends that you had burned. I watched as you restored not only your friends, but Tos as well. I wondered if perhaps you were different from the humans before you, if perhaps you could unite Hilcha. I must however beg forgiveness," the queen said, flying to Chis and landing before him, "for I used you, sweet child, as a pawn. I needed to know that the princess was capable of caring for a fairy as much as she cared for humans. I would not have caused real harm to you, child, yet for the pain I caused you will be rewarded."

Queen Feni flew back to Kuin, not landing, but hovering in front of her and looking her in the eyes. "Your strength is beyond even the greatest stories of this land. You could have killed me, you could have destroyed Dispok and every fairy in it. But you didn't. I pledge to you on this day, all whom I command are at your disposal. We will follow you wherever you lead, and when B'nakma comes, we will lay our lives down to fight for not only Dispok, but the whole of Hilcha. Kse kluf wa gas kmap d'numigba hyi!"

The crowd echoed her last words, chanting them over and over. "Kse kluf wa gas the kmap d'numigba hyi". *We follow you until the forest is no more.*

30

Kuin lay in her bed in the castle of Dispok. It was early morning and the sun was filtering in through her glassless window, the sound of twittering birds softly growing with the light. She had been unable to sleep for more than a couple of hours last night as emotion roiled within her, every feeling being replaced by another before coming back full circle. A knock at her door pulled her from her musings.

"Come," she said, without moving from her bed.

Gungdilkew entered and looked at her. They didn't say anything, they slipped into their more human form and lay beside her. Kuin curled into them, laying her head on their chest.

"Is it less comfortable being like this," she asked, running her hand over their arm.

They shrugged almost imperceptibly. "Not physically, no."

Kuin could feel the non-answer in their answer. "That's not an answer."

They stroked her hair. Even though Kuin wasn't looking at them, she could hear the smile in their voice. "No, I suppose it is not."

A moment passed before they spoke again. "Physically, it makes no difference. It is simply like an article of clothing we can put on as needed," they sighed, "but it is the 'as needed' part that hurts. For so long, my whole life, and my parents before me, humans wouldn't allow us to take part in official meetings unless we were…palatable to them."

Kuin raised her head from their chest and looked at them. "You are beautiful, no matter what form you take. Please don't feel like you ever need to appear a certain way for me."

Gungdilkew shook their head. "No, I do not. But it is much more comfortable for your soft skin," they said, touching her cheek, "to be close to me like this."

Kuin lay her head back on their chest and closed her eyes. "Well, you do feel nice."

There was a comfortable silence that settled, before Kuin spoke again. "I don't know what I'm doing."

Gungdilkew didn't pull back to look at her, simply held her. "How so?"

Kuin's shoulders popped in a shrug. "In any way. I came here because I had nothing on earth. Then B'nakma took Graystone, and my purpose became to save him. But now, after the bridge, after he…" her voice trailed off.

"*He* did not kill your father," Gungdilkew said, stroking her hair. "That was B'nakma."

Kuin's voice cracked. "I know, but what is worse? That I admit that it was B'nakma, and that my brother is gone, or that my brother killed our father? Either way, he is no longer my brother, he is now the enemy. I don't know what to do. I'm just going as the tide pulls me, and now I've been thrust into the role of saving Hilcha; but I don't know how."

"Be you. You are an amazing person, and being you is what has gotten you to this point."

Kuin pulled away from Gungdilkew and stood, looking at them. "An 'amazing person'? My brother is gone because I chose to come here. My father is dead because I chose to leave his home and come here, to

Dispok. My choices caused you and your brother great pain, caused my friend, Bo, great pain. I nearly killed your queen and leveled your kingdom. I'm a terrible person."

As she spoke the last words, her voice broke. She had been thinking it for so long, but voicing it out loud, acknowledging it openly, made it that much more true to her. She slunk down on the floor, buried her face in her hands, and wept.

Gungdilkew slipped down beside her. They didn't try to lift her, nor did they try to remove her face from her hands. They simply sat next to her, shoulders touching.

"No, you are simply a person who was thrust into an impossible world. You learned that you were from another world, you learned that magic wasn't something in storybooks, that you not only have magic but also the blood of the dragon. You were not given a chance to slow down and learn, but instead thrust into a role that you still haven't been prepared for. And yet, despite all of that, you have done the best that you can."

Gungdilkew wrapped their arms around the princess as her chest continued to heave and shudder. "You have shown that you are kind, caring, able to learn from mistakes. You have shown that you have empathy and will do anything for those whom you love."

They now took Kuin's face from her hands, wiping her tears. "You have shown that you are the best of us."

Kuin looked at them. "I feel like I am moving at the speed of light, like by the time I learn how to accept one thing or another, something new is thrown in my lap. I lost my father on that damned bridge, and you know what the messed-up part is? It doesn't hurt anymore. I'm sad for my mother, I'm sad for what may have been with my father, but I didn't know him. I knew Graystone, I loved Graystone like a brother before I even knew that he was, and my soul aches for him. But not my father. What kind of person doesn't mourn their own father?"

"One that didn't get the privilege to know her father. One that spent her whole life believing that her parents had either died or abandoned her. You were dealt a crap hand in life, but you became an amazing person. And you still continue to show that you are someone that deserves to be followed. I knew when you jumped in front of your parents for me, that I would follow you anywhere and I would give anything to be by your side."

Kuin looked at the fairy. Every emotion imaginable ran through her. She was grateful for their friendship, sad that she had hurt them, her heart soared at the thought of the times that they have been there to center her. But something else swelled. A new emotion, one that she had never felt for any boy on earth. Now she felt it for the beautiful fairy that sat beside her.

"Then stay by my side," Kuin said. Before they could answer, she leaned over and put her lips to theirs.

It was a strange feeling, unlike anything she expected for her first kiss. But, she could never have imagined that her first kiss would be the soft, green lips of a fairy. Gungdilkew must have sensed her thoughts, because they pulled away and apologized.

"I'm sorry, I know I'm not-"

Their words were cut off by Kuin's lips again, this time she wrapped her arms around the fairy's neck and pulled them in.

When she finally broke their kiss, she smiled at them. "I'm not sorry," she said, before looking down a bit sheepishly, "unless you didn't want my kiss."

Gungdilkew's answer was to pull her back in.

A few minutes later, a soft knock at the door gave them pause. Kuin giggled as she caught her breath.

"Come," she said, after she and Gungdilkew had separated.

"Oh, I'm sorry, we didn't know you had company," Heekah apologized as she entered the room, Chis clinging to her back.

Chis hopped down and looked back and forth between Kuin and his sibling. "Did you finally kiss her?"

Kuin reddened, Heekah coughed, and Gungdilkew's eyes grew large.

Kuin recovered first, and kneeled down to Chis's height, lowering her voice conspiratorially. "Actually, I kissed them."

Chis beamed. "About time. I'm just a kid, and even I could see you liked each other."

Heekah mercifully changed the subject, though the look on her face told Kuin they would talk about this later. "We were going to go explore the castle, Queen Feni has given us her blessing. We thought the two of you would like to join us. Breakfast will be served in a few hours, and then the queen would like to speak with you, but I thought a bit of exploration might help the time pass until then."

Kuin held out her hand to Gungdilkew. "Join us?"

Gungdilkew smiled at her, as their long twig like fingers twined with hers.

Kuin smiled back, and a few moments later, they were walking through the castle.

The castle was beautiful beyond words. Everything was living, the walls, the floors that they walked on, the stairs that they climbed. Trees tightly grouped together made the walls and floors, moss covering the floors making them soft underfoot. Everything was green, and lush, and alive; and that made Kuin feel alive. She had grown up in a world of concrete and stone. Sure, there were trees in Lorain, a few parks, and even some nice trails. But nothing like this, nothing like the forests she had been awed by since coming here.

And the scent of the castle, fresh and woodsy, was intoxicating. "This is beautiful," she said, after they had walked for only a few moments.

Gungdilkew squeezed her hand. "This is Dispok. And you've barely seen it."

"Then show us," she said, smiling as Chis held on to the former queen's finger.

Her mother had a smile, but sadness was strong in her eyes. Kuin knew that this must be impossibly hard for her, losing her husband and then having to come here and not be given time to mourn. But her mother had done well hiding it, and for now she put the needs of the kingdom before her own.

The castle was beautiful, magnificent and decadent in the most natural way. But it was the grounds that took Kuin's breath away as they walked. Every corner of the land was like the most magnificent garden she had ever seen. Flowers, trees, shrubs, all things natural, grew free; not manicured, but yet not unruly, it was as nature knew when and where to stop growing.

"Do you like it," Chis asked, excitement in his voice.

"It's beautiful," Kuin said.

A small rodent, perhaps a mouse or a chipmunk, scurried away before Kuin could get a good look at it.

Lucky bugger, Bo's smooth purr came in her mind.

Where have you been, Kuin asked, looking around. *In fact, where are you now?*

Bo came walking lazily from behind a bush, stretching in the sunlight, before rubbing himself on her leg. *I've been watching, sneaking around, looking for signs that this is a trap of one kind or another. But I have yet to see any indication that they are being anything but honest with you.*

Kuin reached down and pet his white fur. *Thank you.*

You're welcome, my princess. I, like so many others, will do anything I can to protect you. And here, I'm just a cat. None know who I truly am, and none pay me any mind except to occasionally give me a pet.

Kuin rubbed his head and scratched his chin.

Bo straightened and slipped back into the brush. *I will be here if you need me, princess. For now, I'll be looking to sneak some food from someone.*

Kuin just smiled as he disappeared. The group continued on for a few more minutes, before coming to a small pond. There were benches lining their way around the water, and Kuin sat, the rest following suit a moment later.

Kuin closed her eyes and turned her face to the sun. No one spoke for a few blissful moments. She wished she could stay here, in this place, in this moment, forever. There was no violence threatening her, no looming cost to continue having somewhere to live. Just peace, tranquility, and the smell of nature.

"Lovely, is it not," the voice of Queen Feni came from beside Kuin, and she nearly jumped.

Kuin opened her eyes to see the queen hovering next to her, looking at the lake.

"It is," she answered, her own eyes drifting to the water.

"Princess, I had planned to speak with you at breakfast, but things have come up that will preclude me from joining you for a meal. Can I ask you two questions, and have you answer honestly?"

Kuin turned back to the queen. "I have no reason to lie."

Queen Feni smiled, but it did not reach her eyes. "You have many reasons to lie, and my own bigotry, wrong though it may be, tells me that a human does not need a reason. However, I will ask you anyway and do my best to trust your answers."

Kuin's shoulders popped in a shrug but she said nothing.

"Why did you come here? Not Dispok, but Hilcha?"

Kuin sighed. "That's complicated. At first, because I had nothing left to keep me on Earth."

Kuin went on to explain to her about her life in Lorain, the Palace Theatre, Belly, and everything that led to her agreeing to come here with Bo. She was careful to refer to the cat as Robert, and told the queen that after she got her memories back in Hilcha she never saw the man that brought her here again. Not a total lie.

"But, I suppose the factor that assured that I would come here was Graystone being trapped in his own mind. I would travel to a thousand worlds to try to help him."

Kuin's heart ached at the thought of her brother. Losing her father had hurt, but she barely knew the man; but to have her brother, who's body still worked, who's voice she still heard, trapped in his own mind while B'nakma used him like a marionette, nearly crushed her soul.

The queen hovered before her before landing on a flower on the path before Kuin. "That brings me to my second question. Your brother is gone, the boy that you knew is no more, but his face and body that you have known for so many years belongs to another. And that one, that horrible creature, is the person that you must face to truly unite Hilcha. Are you willing, no, that's not right.

Are you *capable* of ending the life of B'nakma, even if it means killing him when he looks like Graystone? Can you end the life of someone wearing your brother's body like a shell?"

Kuin squeezed her eyes shut as tears ran down her cheeks and dripped from her chin. Knowing that she would not only never speak with her brother again, but she would also have to look into eyes that once belonged to him as she erased all vestiges of him, tore a piece of her very soul away.

"I don't know," she answered, without ever opening her eyes.

She felt a small flutter on her shoulder, and when the queen spoke, she realized that the fairy had landed on her. "Thank you for your honesty. You have the full support of myself and my people. I have already spoken to Gungdilkew, and they will go with you as you travel, they will be my emissary."

"What about Chis," Kuin asked, as the fairy lifted from her shoulder and once again hovered in front of her.

"Chis shall stay here, in Dispok, at my castle, under my care. He will be protected by my own guard, and I will do everything in my power to ensure his safety."

Kuin began to speak, preparing to thank the queen, but the fairy stopped her.

"People are going to die, Princess Kuin, humans, fairies, and every species that will stand with you against the darkness. You will lose friends; you have already lost family. This land will suffer, and the time for mourning when it is all over will come. But you must be focused on defeating B'nakma. Not everyone, even in the human court, can be trusted. You will need to push down your pain, push down your sorrow and your loss, bury all of those things until you have met your goal. Until you have freed this land, and banished B'nakma for a final time. Then, all of us will come together and help one another heal in the same way that we will band together to help save our lands and freedom. If you are strong, we will once again be united and we will all follow a great dragon-blooded human queen."

After she finished speaking, the queen landed on the ground before Kuin and kneeled. Kuin fought back more tears at Queen Feni's words, the true weight of her responsibility, of her purpose here settling on her shoulders.

"Then let us," she said, rising and holding out her hand to the queen, "lead the fight."

Queen Feni landed in her hand and smiled, and the princess simply smiled back, hope strong in both of their smiles.

31

Kuin barely ate breakfast that morning, her mind on what she would need to do. Seated at the table with her were her mother, Gungdilkew, and Chis. The queen, true to her word, had been unable to join them.

"Mother," she said, lifting her eyes from her plate.

Heekah looked at her daughter, as the entire table came to a hush.

"I am sorry that you lost father."

Heekah put her fork down, dabbing at her mouth with a napkin of tightly woven green. "Thank you. We all knew the risks when we left our home, and there will be time for me, us, to properly mourn your father."

Kuin nodded. "Yes. But we have to go to other peoples, talk to other species, and if you would rather stay here where you are safe, I would not object."

I *want* you to stay here, I want you safe so that I have at least one parent to get to know, Kuin thought.

"I would dishonor your father if I did not fight beside you, whether with words in the courts of other castles, or when the time comes, on the battlefield," Heekah said with a sigh. "Nowhere is safe, there will be danger even here eventually. I would rather be by your side."

Kuin nodded, both concerned and proud of her mother at the same time. "That is your choice to make. I want to leave as soon as the sun comes up tomorrow."

Kuin looked at Gungdilkew, then Chis. "Chis," she started, but the young fairy cut her off.

"I know, you guys get to go, and I have to stay here," he said, sounding not a little pouty.

Kuin stood and went to his side, kneeling next to his chair. "It's beautiful here, and I know that Queen Feni will keep you plenty busy with fun things. And we," she said, glancing to the other two, "will be back before you know it."

Chis cocked his head and smiled at her. "Will you give me a dragon ride when you come back?"

It was Heekah that answered. "Why wait," she said with a smile, scooping the young fairy up and setting him on her shoulders before running out of the room.

When Kuin laughed at the sight, Gungdilkew smiled at her. "I've never heard you laugh like that before."

Kuin looked at them. "Things have been difficult since I got here. I guess I don't have much time to laugh."

They stood and walked to Kuin, preparing to take her hand. Before they could, however, the princess went rigid, and lifted from the floor.

"Go next to Yilo, the Centaurs, convince them to join your cause, young emissary. Stand by your princess and watch as she saves not only your people but all. But there is always a cost to victory, and defeating the dark God will be no different. The fate of one, or the future of all."

Kuin lowered back to the ground, her feet finding purchase and she did not fall this time. With every event, she became more stable, more able to handle the magic that coursed through her.

"What did I say," she asked.

Gungdilkew repeated her words back to her, and she just stood there for a moment.

"I will not survive this, you know that right," Kuin asked, head down, eyes closed.

Gungdilkew took her hands in their own. "We do not know what the prophesy means. We do not even know where they are coming from. Have faith."

Kuin looked up at them, tears filling her eyes but not spilling. "I will die. What else could it mean? But I'm not scared of that. I'm not even mad that I came to this world just to die. I've found so much here and have lost so much here as well. But I've found purpose and peace, peace despite the coming war, peace at knowing who I am and that I am not just an orphan living in a dusty attic stealing to survive, and," she looked at Gungdilkew for a moment. "And something more."

The fairy squeezed the princesses' hands gently, and leaned in and kissed her cheek. "And I am glad that you have."

***

That night, they packed their few belongings and prepared to leave at first light. Before she could lie down, there was a soft knock on Kuin's door.

"Come," she said, pulling a blanket around her nightclothes.

A fairy that she recognized as one of the queen's guards, one that she had knocked unconscious with her power in the courtyard only a day ago, came in and bowed deeply.

"Princess Kuin, I have word from the Queen."

Kuin just nodded, and the guard continued.

"Queen Feni sends her regrets that she will not be here to see you off in the morning. She received urgent news just this morning of a situation, and she must attend to it. She asks that you forgive her absence, and offers you this gift," the guard said, coming in a bit farther and setting a small box of perfectly polished dark wood on the table next to her bed.

"She also asks that you keep the young fairy safe, and she promises that she will see you when the time is right."

Kuin nodded, and the guard turned to leave. Just as he began to close the door behind him, she spoke.

"What is your name?"

The guard paused, before turning and bowing again. "I am called Klol, your royal highness."

Kuin closed the distance to the fairy and took his hand. "Klol, I am Kuin. There is no need for you to use my title. Please allow me to apologize for yesterday."

The guard cocked his head. "There is no need for an apology. You reacted admirably to protect those that you cared for."

Kuin smiled softly. "Well, just the same."

The guard returned her smile, before bowing again and leaving.

Kuin went to the box that the guard had left. Kuin lifted the lid and gasped at what lay inside. A ring of the same dark wood as the box lay upon a soft pad of moss. The ring bore the carving of a dragon battling alongside fairies, the two coming together to face off against the shadowy shape of a human. The detail in the piece drew her in, and she could have sworn that she saw smoke swirl at the end of the dragon's nostrils and feel heat from the wood. The sensation left just as quickly as it had come. A small note was nestled into the lid of the box.

Princess Kuin, First of Your Name, please accept this ring as a token of our alliance. With Gungdilkew by your side, and this ring on your finger, may no one doubt that the fairies of Dispok stand with you. And if you should find yourself in need, use this ring, for it is carved from no simple tree, but from the great tree of our ancestor, Ngwok, and within it sings the powerful magic of our land.

Queen Feni

Kuin slid the ring onto her pointer finger, and she felt the hum of the magic within it course through her, before being absorbed. Kuin held her hand up and examined the piece, and while its carving was just as beautiful as before, it no longer seemed to roil with heat and smoke; it now appeared to be just a ring.

Kuin felt for her powers, embraced them as she did, but they felt no different than before. She couldn't help but wish that the queen would have left instructions on how to use whatever power it had gifted her.

As she lay down for the night, her eyes closing, she swore she could feel the lush bed wrap around her in a soft embrace.

32

The next morning, after quick breakfast, Kuin, Heekah, and Gungdilkew, said their goodbyes, and headed south to Yilo. What would have been a journey of at least two days on foot, was made shorter by the horses which Queen Feni provided for them. Kuin had never ridden before, despite her love of the animal growing up. She found them majestic and beautiful, but Lorain didn't provide many places for a housing challenged girl as she had been to learn to ride. Her mother had agreed to ride with her, and for hours they pushed on, the sun rising higher in the sky, before slowly beginning its decent once more.

"I had hoped to get to Yilo by nightfall," Heekah said, slowing the horse. "But I don't think we can, and if we do manage to, the hour will still be late, and the Centaurs are not known for their hospitality."

"What do you suggest," Gungdilkew asked, pulling their horse in stride with Heekah's.

"We should find a place to make camp. There are caves here that I've used before when I was younger, I'm sure many of them still are suitable."

After another hour's ride, they indeed found a cave wide and open in the prairie.

"There are no wolves in them, are there," Kuin asked skeptically as she dismounted her mother's horse, before holding out her hand to assist the other woman down.

Heekah shook her head, and looked behind her to the nearly set sun. The sky was an inferno of red, orange, and purple colors. "No, not that I am aware of. They were used by smugglers in another time, but when I was queen and trade was open and free, they were no longer necessary. However, they aren't natural, that much is clear. They were carved from the Hilcha, and for what purpose originally, we will likely never know."

"Where will we tie off the horses for the night," Kuin asked, looking around at the empty and open flatlands around them.

"They will not wander off. Dispokian horses are well trained, and know not to leave their riders side," Gungdilkew said, rubbing the flank of their own beast. As if in answer, the horse nuzzled its head into their neck.

Heekah grabbed her tuck and beckoned Kuin to do the same. They took their few belongings into the cave, the nearly faded daylight only penetrating a few feet into the hollow.

"I didn't pack a torch," Kuin said.

Without a word, her mother cast a ball of warm red-orange flame above them. The ball rose to the ceiling, perhaps ten or fifteen feet, Kuin couldn't be sure. Quickly, the light shot deeper into the cave and Kuin ran after it, not wanting to be left in darkness.

Heekah let out a small laugh, and called after her. "It will only go far enough ahead of you to light the way. When the gwu, the flame, reaches the edge of illumination for our path it will stop until we catch up."

Kuin stopped, and as if to prove her mother right, the flame halted as well. Kuin whirled on her mother, and the ball of flame flew in an instant from one end of the path back to where it had come, light once again revealing Heekah and Gungdilkew.

"You don't need to laugh at me," Kuin snapped, hoping that the redness of her embarrassed flush would not be visible in the light of the ball of flame.

Heekah walked a bit quicker now, closing the twenty or so feet between them in an instant. "I wasn't laughing at you, I'm sorry. I wouldn't laugh at you, wugb."

Wugb. Daughter. It was the first time that her mother had used that word when talking to her and a small bit of her irritation melted. "Yet you did," she answered, embarrassment and anger still heating enough of her to not allow her to let it go.

Kuin didn't know why it bothered her that her mother had laughed. It hadn't been malicious; the older woman was likely telling the truth when she said she wasn't laughing *at* her. Her anger cooled to irritation, and she turned and began walking further into the cave again, the enchanted flame launching itself back so that it stayed in front of her.

One of the things that Kuin had appreciated about this journey that they had been on, was the chance to not be stuck in her parents' house, nothing but the reminders of what had been stolen from her in every corner. She had been given the opportunity to see new places, meet new people, flex her powers, and not be smothered by her parents.

Her parents. The thought caused Kuin to pause her walking. She had wished her whole life for parents that loved her, and when she had been given that gift, she had been nothing but bitter, angry with them. Not with them, she knew, but with having what should have been ripped away and replaced by a childhood of being unhoused and having to steal to survive.

Her thoughts drifted to her father, to the image of him being thrown over the edge of the bridge by Graystone, or at least by the dark God that controlled his body. Guilt coursed through her at the fact that she would never have the chance to be a better daughter to Fyan, never have the chance to even truly get to know him. Her eyes dampened, but at the sound of Heekah and Gungdilkew's footsteps approaching from behind her she dragged the back of her hand across her eyes and began to walk again.

As if reading her mind, Heekah spoke, her words nearly causing the tears that had threatened a second before to spill like water over a burst dam. "He loved you too."

Kuin didn't acknowledge her mother, didn't say a word as her two companions walked softly past her and continued pressing forward into the cave, Gungdilkew drawing a gentle hand across her arm as they walked past.

Kuin reached out and took their hand, lacing her fingers with their twig-like digits. Gungdilkew glanced at her but said nothing as she drew close to him and they continued down that path and farther into the cave.

The path ended in a horseshoe, smooth stone walls curving in a semi-circle leaving the only way out to trace their steps back.

"This will work," Heekah said, letting her tuck slide from her shoulder gently to the ground.

Kuin and Gungdilkew did the same, Gungdilkew reaching in a grabbing a couple of small berry loaves, unwrapped the leaves that had protected them, and offered them to the women. Kuin and Heekah both accepted and began eating them; the group quiet save for the sound of them chewing.

Kuin thought of Glem as she ate her loaf. He had been so excited to try the berry loaves, and he had enjoyed them greatly. Now, the memory of the man whom she watched get thrown from the bridge with her father soured the taste of the berry in her mouth.

Kuin wrapped the loaf in the leaves that Gungdilkew had taken it from, and set it down next to her. She hoped that the dim light from the enchanted orb that her mother had produced did not reveal the tears again pricking at the edges of her eyes.

"He was a good man, Glem," Gungdilkew said, their smile soft in the red light. "He lived a life serving the Mothers, and he will be remembered as a hero when this is written in history."

Kuin scoffed. "History will write what it will, and if we fail, then he will go down as a fool that was thrown off of a bridge."

Heekah looked to her daughter. For a moment, Kuin held her gaze before dropping her eyes to her lap. "Is that what you think of Wise Glem," her mother asked.

Kuin just shrugged.

Heekah sighed. "Glem was a Wise, he had courage and strength beyond many men."

Heekah stretched out onto the stone floor of the cave, placing her tuck under her head as a pillow. Kuin and Gungdilkew followed suit, and soon the enchanted light extinguished, and the sound of snoring filled the hollow darkness.

***

Kuin couldn't move. She opened her eyes but saw nothing. Her world was pitch black, darkness like that of B'nakma surrounded her. She got her bearings quickly; she was in the cave; she could hear the sound of her mother and Gungdilkew breathing steadily. There were no other sounds, but Kuin could feel her skin crawl. Something was wrong. Something was there, with them, in the cave. She tried to sit up, but she couldn't move. Panic struck her, and she opened her mouth to scream, but only the soft breathing of her companions filled the air. She had to do something.

A skittering sound closer to the entrance caught her attention, and she tried to turn her head to look despite the pitch black. But she couldn't move, couldn't scream, couldn't do anything but lay there and listen as the sound drew closer to them.

***

Graystone had watched quietly in B'nakma's mind for what felt like a lifetime. The dark God had thought that he had snuffed the boy out, thought that he had pushed out the last of his consciousness and consumed his body wholly.

But Graystone still lived there, in the deep recesses of the body he had been born into. Watching, listening, in silence. He had stopped trying to speak, stopped trying to move. At first he had been afraid to even think, B'nakma would surely hear any thoughts he had, and would end his life completely.

But B'nakma hadn't heard his thoughts; indeed, B'nakma had seemed content that Graystone was in fact gone, and he no longer shielded his thoughts and mind from the boy.

Graystone had watched as Kuin, her mother, and the fairy had emerged from the blind spot that was Dispok. Watched as they had ridden until evening before taking refuge in a cave for the night. Graystone had seen the images in B'nakma's mind of what lay in that cave, he had watched as B'nakma relived his first encounter with the creature. Fearsome and strong, the creature had nearly defeated B'nakma before the dark God trapped and enslaved it. When B'nakma had weakened, the creature was able to escape its shackles and return to its home. B'nakma still craved its power, wanted it for his army, Graystone could feel the desire coursing through the God inhabiting his body; but B'nakma was as yet too weak to battle the creature, and he was confident that he would snuff out Kuin's life quickly and easily without the need for help from the beings of Hilcha.

Something in the cave stopped B'nakma, and thus Graystone, from being able to see what was happening inside of it. An impenetrable haze shielded the entrance from B'nakma's prying gaze, and as the God went about his business, Graystone retreated back into near nothingness.

33

Bo had spent so much time in human form, that when he returned to Hilcha and was once again blessed with four legs and a tail, he had wanted nothing more than to run off and chase mice and bugs, lounge in the green grass under the warm sun, and maybe come back around to his humans for a rub or two when he was feeling lonely.

It had surprised the cat when he hadn't been able to do just that. After years spent searching for the girl, for his Kuin, and finding her and her brother, he found that wandering too far from her made him anxious. Anxious! He was a cat, anxiety over a human's well being was not something he was used to or desirous of. Yet, here he was, following behind his family and Gungdilkew from a distance, never too far, but always trying to enjoy just being a cat while still keeping close enough to listen in on Kuin and Heekah's journey through the collar that the Mothers had gifted him.

Bo had not felt emotion through the collar, only heard conversations and thoughts between Heekah and Kuin. But as he stalked a rodent through the grass outside of the cave, fear gripped him. He knew it wasn't his fear, and it took him only a second or two to place it as Kuin's fear.

Kuin, what is happening? What's wrong?

Bo tried to speak to his princess, asking again and again through the magic of his collar what was happening,

but he received no response. Much like Kuin in the cave,
he was gripped with fear, unable to make his body move.
A dread as he had never known held him tight, standing
under the moonlight in the grass of the plain like a white
marble cat statue.

Kuin heard her friend turned cat in her mind, calling
for her, reaching for her. She heard the panic in his voice
steadily rise as he said he couldn't move, didn't know
where she was, couldn't help her.

But everything faded from her mind as the creature
she had heard crawled into the dim light of the cave. She
had barely been able to see before her eyes adjusted, and
now she wished she couldn't. A spider, nearly as big as
Chis, crawled up her leg and sat on her torso, eight beady
eyes staring directly into hers. Venom dripped from the
fangs on either side of its head.

Who are you?

The voice was small and scratchy, almost a hiss in
Kuin's mind. Kuin didn't answer, frozen in fear and not
entirely sure that it was speaking to her.

The spider tapped her forehead with one of its front
legs. *You, tiny human, who are you?*

I…I'm not tiny.

The spider's body shook just a little, and Kuin
thought it was going to attack her for an instant before the
voice in her head chuckled, and she realized the spider
was laughing.

*I'm just a baby, and I'm half as big as you are.
When I'm your age, I'll be three or four times your size.*

So, yes, you are tiny. But that isn't the important part of this; who are you?

Kuin found enough strength to lift her head, looking for Gungdilkew and her mother. Both were still sleeping. *I am Kuin, but just a nobody. Is this your cave?*

The spider's body shook again. *A nobody? The princess is humble, I guess. And yes, this is our home.*

Kuin raised an eyebrow. *Our?*

Yes, the spider hissed in her mind, *our. My mother, and all of my siblings.*

Kuin did not want to think of more 'baby' spiders this size sharing the cave with them, let alone how large the mother must be. *I'm sorry that we intruded. I…we will leave now, if you would like. We didn't know that you were here.*

The spider put its two front legs down on either side of Kuin's head. *I don't want you to leave. I want to help you. My mother says that we owe you.*

Kuin didn't know what to make of that. The spiders…owed her? How? Why? And for what?

Before Kuin could answer, a dagger gleaned for just a moment in the dim light, before plunging into the neck of the spider. Kuin jumped up, the spider dropping to the ground squealing and writhing in pain. Her mother grabbed her and dragged her away from the creature.

"We need to go; now," her mother said, as Gungdilkew jumped up.

The sound of something coming from the direction of the entrance of the cave caused the three of them to turn. Heekah held her arm out and stood in front of Kuin.

"Get behind me," the older woman said, holding her dagger in front of them.

Bo came bounding into the opening. Heekah relaxed as the cat spoke.

I would prefer not to be stabbed today, your highness.

Heekah smiled and bent over to pat the cat on the head before running out of the room they were in. They almost made it to the path when a spider the size of at least four or five people descended down a web in front of them.

The spider dropped in front of them and regarded them with all eight of it's eyes, as the squeals of the young spider still echoed behind them.

What did you do, a much older and even more terrifying voice hissed into Kuin's mind.

I saved my daughter, Heekah responded, apparently linked to the voice as well.

My son was no threat to your daughter. He was foolish to approach you, yes, but he would not have harmed any of you.

Heekah didn't care to debate with the deadly creature. Instead, heat rose in her, and she flung out flames.

The spider shrank back, squealing, and Heekah grabbed her daughter's hand and ran from the cave, Gungdilkew and Bo right behind them.

Just as the cave's entrance came into view, the first rays of sun casting an orange and pink hue, Kuin froze.

Heekah jerked to a stop, Kuin's hand still in hers. "What are you doing?"

But Kuin couldn't answer. In her mind she was seeing what the mother spider saw, her child in a pool of blood, slowly dying, its squeals turned to weak whimpers. She could feel the mother's sadness, her pure and raw desperation.

My baby, my sweet baby, no. Please no, the mother cried as she picked the young spider up in her front legs and cradled it.

Kuin ripped her hand from her mother's, and turned back, sprinting deeper into the cave. She saw the mother holding her baby, heard its weeping in her mind. As Kuin dropped to her knees at their feet, the mother finally noticed her.

Kuin felt the mother's emotion switch from sadness and loss, to white hot rage. *Have you come to kill me as well? You will find I am not nearly as vulnerable as my son was.*

The massive creature set her child down gently, and in an instant was towering above Kuin, its venomous jaws on either side of its head raining poison down around her.

Even as Kuin's heart raced in fear, she could feel the life of the small spider still draining; its final vestiges slipping away.

Kuin stood from her knees, her eyes inches from the crouched mother spider's. "He yet lives. Let me save him," she said out loud.

Several of the spider's eyes spun to look at her baby. *He is already gone. You humans killed him. The only reason that you yet live is because I owe you a debt.*

There it was again, talk of a debt that was owed from the spiders to Kuin. But she did not have time to think about that. *He is not dead yet. Please, please, let me save him,* Kuin begged into the spider's mind.

After a second's hesitation, the giant arachnid stepped back and Kuin rushed to the baby.

Kuin pulled him in close, and reached for her power. Red hot heat began to burn in her, and she reached deeper. White flame encompassed both her and the baby spider, its wound closing, its heart once again beating. The baby's eyes began moving, searching. *Wha…what happ…what happened?*

Kuin did not let her magic go, the cave bright in the light of her white flame. *Humans happened. As always, humans happened. And I am sorry.*

The spider looked at her, query in its eyes. *But you saved me. Humans are good too, like every creature. And to be fair, I probably shouldn't have even shown myself to you. Mother said you would likely be scared of me.*

Kuin released her power, the cave again dark in its absence. She thought about what her mother had done earlier, and she formed a small ball of flame, casting it up to illuminate the cave. It wasn't as strong, nor as steady, as her mothers, but it pierced the darkness just the same.

And I was right, his mother's voice said. The giant spider hunched down and touched its head to her baby's for a moment, before turning to Kuin.

In what Kuin could only call a bow, it supplicated itself before her. *Mistakes were made by both of us, Princess Kuin, first of your name, but I am not your enemy, nor are any of my children. You have my kingdom at your disposal in the coming war.*

Heekah's voice, out loud for the benefit of Gungdilkew, rang out in the cave. "May we have your name, queen?"

Gungdilkew gasped at the question. They knew the lore, the stories, the tales of old, but none believed them anymore. They couldn't hear the queens response, but they knew it just the same.

The queen spider stood to her full height, tall and proud over them. *I am Brimda, fourteenth of my name, daughter of Brimda, mother to Brimda, Queen of the kingdom of Bnem, the kingdom of all things crawling and slithering across and under Hilcha.*

Kuin dropped to her knee in the same respect that Brimda had just shown her, Heekah, Gungdilkew and even Bo followed suit and kneeled before the Queen of Bnem.

Stand, Princess Kuin and Queen Heekah, stand Gungdilkew of the fairies, stand Robert Steekus, goodest of the good boys.

When the group rose, the Queen Brimda spoke again. *I would ask that you spend a few more hours in our company, but I would ask that you follow us into our home. I want to tell you why we owe both Kuin and Heekah a debt we may never be able to repay, and we will allow you to decide if you shall forgive our transgression, or exact your revenge.*

34

Where Kuin and her group had slept had seemed like a dead-end last night, but Queen Brimda led them through a split in the rock wall that was easily missed if they didn't know where to look.

This way, the queen said, guiding them deeper and deeper into the cave. The path was wide enough for them to all walk side by side behind the queen, sloping down as they walked, and the only light was the magic light that Heekah had once again cast above them, until finally a light was visible at the end of the passage.

As they got closer, the air became much fresher than the stagnant air of the cave, and a light breeze blew along the path. When they reached the end of the path it opened into a massive cave.

Kuin gasped at the sight, Gungdilkew took a deep breath and let it out slowly, savoring the earthy air.

The ceiling of the cave was open, high enough above them that Kuin thought any of the buildings in Cleveland could have easily fit between the grass covered bed and the edge of the opening high above; trees, shrubs, flowers, and grass covered the ground. The early sunlight filtering in through the treetop canopy was warm and inviting. Kuin tried to see the other side of the great circle of greenery, but the trees were so dense that she didn't know how far it stretched.

"This is incredible," Heekah said out loud.

Gungdilkew just stared in awe. Bo took a look around and began wandering away.

I won't be far, the cat said for Kuin and her mother to hear. He glanced over his shoulder at them and then took off, disappearing into the wood.

We are almost there, Brimda said to Heekah and Kuin, and Kuin relayed the words to Gungdilkew. They simply nodded, still awestruck by the sight of a lush forest at the heart of the cave.

An outline of a building began to take shape in the distance, and as they neared, Kuin could see it was a home. She guessed from the outside that it was big enough for one or two people to live comfortably in. "What is this place," she asked as Brimda led them to the structure.

Before Queen Brimda could respond, Heekah practically whispered the answer to her daughter's question. "Hab".

"Hab? Hab is a myth, a legend, it's the stuff we tell children to keep them in line," Gungdilkew said, raising an eyebrow.

Heekah shook her head. "No. I've seen drawings, I've seen the royal records, handwritten accounts from my ancestors, passed down for generations."

Kuin sighed. "Can someone please tell me what 'Hab' is?"

Hab is the place where we once met with humans, fae, and every other sentient species that roam Hilcha. We were once a valued part of this world, respected and respectful. Until…

Queen Brimda's voice trailed off in Kuin's mind. "Until Slihul turned on the guests here," Heekah finished.

Kuin was exasperated; every answer seemed to create more questions.

"The stories are true then," Gungdilkew asked in awe.

The stories are many, some are true, most are not. But yes, Slihul turned on our honored guests, slaughtering not only the leaders of the other races, but also their families that had come with them. Slihul dishonored us, and we killed her for her actions. But from that day we were to be forever feared and reviled. We have never been able to return to the outside world, our numbers have shrunk to a fraction of what we once were, our kingdom is no longer a kingdom. We are but a clan, a small family really, and we simply survive here and rarely wander out to seek food. I, myself, in fact, have not let the safety of this cave for nearly four decades.

Kuin told Gungdilkew what the Queen said, and they looked back toward the small home, jaw slack in awe.

Kuin looked at Brimda's eyes. "Why did you bring us here?"

As if snapping a trance away, Gungdilkew and Heekah both turned and faced the spider queen, curious what the answer was.

We owe you, Princess Kuin, first of your name, and you, Queen Heekah, a debt. Nearly fifteen years ago, we were approached by a person that we thought was a representative of you, Queen Heekah. We had been out of practice with humans, with their language, with their tells when they lie, with just how easily, in fact, they do lie. Needless to say, we were excited by her words.

"I didn't think this place was real, let alone think of sending an envoy," Heekah said, curiosity sparked.

Indeed, Queen Brimda continued, with what could only be described as a nodding of her body. *We figured that out, but far too late. The woman who came to us, who found us and asked us for our assistance was, in fact, an emissary of B'nakma. But, to us her words seemed genuine. She spoke of us doing the kingdom of man a great favor. She claimed that B'nakma was nearly full strength again, and back in physical form. She told us that war was imminent, and begged us to assist in protecting you, Princess Kuin.*

"What did she ask of you," Kuin asked, her mind already knowing, but not ready to accept.

She told us that the Queen, the spider turned briefly towards Heekah before returning her gaze to Kuin, *had requested that we take her child to a secret place for protection, and that we should take the queen's stepson as well for he was in danger just the same. She told us to deliver the children to the guards that would be waiting, and we would have restored our honor amongst the humans.*

Kuin glanced at her mother. The older woman's expression was tight, but anger and pain shone through. "And so, you stole us away?"

The queen's body bobbed up and down in what Kuin assumed was a nod. *Yes, of course. Had I been thinking, really thinking, I would've questioned so much of her story. But I wasn't thinking. I saw a way for us to repair our relationship with Hilcha, to emerge from our cave, leave the darkness of Hab, and perhaps even thrive again. I was thinking of my own children, and the future they could have, the possibility to be the first generation in dozens of generations to be free of Hab, to have honor. Alas, instead I only brought further shame onto my family and our kind.*

Heekah spoke, her words clipped and precise. "No one can blame you for wanting better for your children and your kingdom, but how could you not come to tell us? How could you leave my husband," her voice cracked at the mention of him, "and I not knowing where our daughter was, or if she was even alive?"

Gungdilkew started to ask Kuin what the queen was saying, but they were silenced by a look from her when they opened their mouth.

Kuin turned to Brimda. "Will you answer my mother's question?"

I will. Shame, shame and fear is all I can offer as an excuse. I have lived with the shame of knowing who stole your children, the spider faced Heekah now, queen to queen. But let me ask you, if our roles were reversed, would you have done differently? Would you risk the life of the princess and all of your people, in order to have a clear conscience?

When Heekah just stared at her, Brimda continued. *We have to make very difficult decisions, you and I, and one day your daughter when she is queen, but we do what we believe to be in the best interests of our families and our kingdoms. I did no different. I do not ask you to spare my life for what I have done, I ask only that you allow my family to live. They will not leave Hab, they will not wander into the world of Hilcha, but please let them live. The decision was mine alone, and I ask you, queen to queen, punish me and not them.*

Kuin could see her mother's face darken, she swore she could almost see flame in her mother's eyes, and so she jumped in before her mother could respond.

As I was one of the two taken, and the other is not here to speak, I tell you, no harm will come to your family. You made a terrible mistake, one that cost my family, my kingdom, and possibly this entire world, dearly; a foolish, greedy choice that you will pay for, but your children and your kingdom should not.

Heat rose in Kuin as thought about the life she could have had, the life she should have had. Anger flared when she thought of her brother, somewhere in the claws of an evil god, if he even yet lived. Her eyes were bright red with flame and heat as she let her power flow and released her flame on the Queen.

$$35$$

Queen Brimda squealed and writhed as the flames engulfed her. Except, they didn't engulf her. In fact, she realized that the pain was in only one place, her middle leg on her left side. Kuin stopped the flame, and it coiled back into her.

You did not harm my family with intent. You did so with negligence, you did so with the hope that what you were doing would repair your stance in the world of Hilcha. Your true fault, the reason for your pain, is that you never told my mother of what you had done. Had you done so, and done so immediately, perhaps I would have been found sooner.

Kuin heard the sounds of other spiders, Brimda's children, squealing softly, in sympathy for their mother, in fear for themselves. She reached for the white heat of her healing, and released it upon the spider queen.

My pain was temporary, as was my parents, but the scars will last until my mother and I die, and sadly did last for my father until the day he died. Kuin walked directly next to the queen and placed her hand on the burned leg. *So to, your pain need not be long, but you will live with the scars upon your leg for all of your days, as a reminder of what you did and a reminder to make better choices in the future.*

Queen Brimda lowered her front legs, bowing to Kuin. *And your understanding and mercy will give you our respect and support from this day until the last dragon rests forever. The Myisbe will always answer your call, Princess Kuin, first of your name.*

Kuin looked at the queen for a moment, before nodding. "And you will be called upon," she said out loud before looking back at the small hut in the clearing.

This place, Kuin asked, gesturing around them, *is B'nakma able to see what happens here?*

It was Heekah that answered. *No, this place is shielded from his magic, from anyone on the outside's magic in fact.*

Kuin smiled. "Good, very good," she said, before telling the queen, and her companions, what her plan was.

If spiders could smile, Kuin was certain that Brimda would be sharing her dark smile when she finished laying things out for the queen.

Very wise, princess. But, before you go, please accept a token of my children's gratitude. They have made it while we speak. They were afraid that their mother would leave them this day, and want you to have this so that you never forget that they are grateful for your mercy.

A young spider came and set down a small item in the grass at Kuin's feet. She picked it up. "It is beautiful," she said, looking at the sparkling silken ring; golden silk, blended with the darkest black and a single string of fire red than twisted through the ring. "Thank you, all of you."

May it serve you well, and allow it to serve as a reminder that we will serve you well also.

Bo silently reappeared from the forest of Hab, sitting himself at the feet of Kuin. *Princess, with the permission of Queen Brimda, I would like to stay here in Hab until you come this way again.*

Kuin didn't know when she would be passing by, but she didn't mind the cat staying if that was what suited him.

The princess kneeled down and rubbed the cat's head, Bo purring softly into her as he sat there. "If Queen Brimda does not mind, you have my permission."

It would be our honor. Please, make Hab your home for as long as you would like.

Kuin gave Bo one more round of scratches on his head, and turned to leave.

B'nakma sat in silence, watching in frustration as the blasted princess and her companions did not leave the cave. They had been inside all night, and the sun had come up with still no sign of them. Fear struck the god of darkness at the idea that perhaps the cursed spiders had rid him of the joy of killing them. He had sent his crone, Yaswi, to capture the princess and kill the others if they tried to interfere.

The dark god's heart raced when he once again saw the forms of the princess, her mother, and the fairy. Anger flashed in him as he realized that they were fleeing, hundreds of young spiders pouring from the mouth of the cave as they ran, sticky webs launching at them, but the group managed to stay just out of the range of the silk netting. His anger waned as he watched the spiders give up and scurry back into their cave home. Good, he would have the privilege of killing them.

***

Yaswi had watched the entrance of the cave all night, and as the sun had rose, all morning. Adrenaline coursed through her as she saw the princess and her group come rushing out of the cave. She hid as the spiders gave chase, prepared to strike when she watched the spiders retreat.

The princess was at the very front of the group, leading the exodus, her mother behind her, with Gungdilkew running right behind them.

Yaswi summoned her power and rose from her hiding place in the tall grass of the plains.

"Princess," the old crone shrieked, "the master would like a word with you."

The group came to an abrupt stop twenty or so feet from her.

"Yaswi," Heekah called out, "is that you, or are you simply the shell inhabited by the demon?"

The crone smiled a wicked smile, revealing crooked and sharp teeth. "Hello, Queen. Is that how you speak to your dear aunty?"

Dark smoke roiled from the demon's hands as she raised them, and the sun went dark. Kuin took a step back as the smoke rolled along the ground and rose before them. There was something mesmerizing about the smoke, something that made her unable to do anything but watch it. The princess watched as hands formed in the smoke and reached for her.

"No," her mother yelled out, before Kuin could even react.

Heekah shoved her daughter behind her, and the hands wrapped around the woman's neck. As suddenly as the demon crone had appeared only moments ago, the smoke, the demon, and Heekah were gone.

Kuin screamed, not a fearful scream, but a scream of equal parts rage and loss. Gungdilkew wrapped their arms around the princess, and she wept into them. "He has killed my father and taken my mother," she sobbed as the fairy rubbed her hair. "He has Graystone, if my brother yet lives. I was given a family only to have it ripped from me."

Gungdilkew just held the princess, and let her sob into them for as long as she needed.

B'nakma roared and smashed the desk at which he sat. That wretched demon had failed him again. She was to bring him the princess, and yet she had brought the queen. A queen whose magic did him no good, and who served little purpose to him. Perhaps he could use her as a bargaining chip, but he doubted that Kuin would trade herself for her mother.

"My lord," Yaswi started, but her words were cut off by an inhuman shriek when B'nakma sent sharp blades of power through her mind.

The dark god stood and walked slowly over to where the demon contorted and writhed on the floor of his study.

"What were your orders?"

"I was…to get the…princess and deliver her…to you," Yaswi struggled through the pain.

B'nakma looked to the unconscious queen who lay on the floor next to Yaswi. "I was under the impression that the Princess was only fourteen years old. Have I been mistaken? Have I not known the face of the one that I pursue?"

Fear caused Yaswi to begin sobbing. The demon was embarrassed to be in such a position; it knew that its master was disappointed and angered but the demon had hoped that the queen would be good enough.

A new round of pain coursed through the demon, and B'nakma smiled wickedly. "I have had enough of your failure. I wish I could dispose of you now, but I feel like you may have some use. So instead, I shall trap you in your own mind until I find a purpose for you again. I will torment you with pure pain until then."

B'nakma snapped his fingers, and laughed as Yaswi went still and silent.

He lifted the demon's body easily, taking it to one of the many unused bed chambers in his castle, and tossing it onto the ground. He didn't bother to put the demon in a bed, but he did at least spark a fire in the hearth so that the body wouldn't freeze solid.

The god of darkness walked back to his study, and looked his prisoner up and down. The former queen remained unconscious, but he would wake her soon. He would enjoy torturing her, knowing even so that she would likely have no information to offer him. But, perhaps holding her would give him some leverage over Princess Kuin.

36

Heekah opened her eyes and saw nothing; silence and pitch black were the only things that her senses revealed to her. It wasn't quiet, the kind of quiet where there is still some sort of ambient noise, a rustle in the trees from the wind, a bird chirping in the distance. No, this was the kind of complete silence that leaves your mind creating sounds, making your ears ring, just to keep you from going mad.

She tried to speak, but she couldn't move. Aside from her eyes, none of her muscles responded to her orders. She moved her eyes in every direction, hoping for the smallest glimmer of light, but saw nothing.

Finally, a voice broke the silence, a soft but evil whisper of a hiss. "Hello, queen."

"B'nakma."

"Yes, finally we meet. How is your husband?"

Heekah spewed a string of curses before B'nakma spoke again.

"I understand you're upset, queen, but I assure you, I take no joy in dragging this out. It was supposed to be your daughter here before me. Yaswi, or the demon that inherits her body as she is long gone, failed me, and brought you instead. Now, I have no real use for you, other than perhaps trading you for your daughter."

"Leave my daughter alone. Why do you want her anyway? You stole her away from me, but then abandoned her on another world? Why? Why not just kill her then?"

B'nakma debated for a moment on whether or not to reveal his plan to the former queen. But he decided that since she wouldn't be leaving this castle alive, and he was tired of speaking only to his demons, he would tell her.

"Your bloodline and mine have always been intertwined. The Mother's choice to go dormant was in order to rob me of my power. We are connected, they are a light to my darkness. Unlike them, however, I was not willing to lay quietly and allow the world to go on around us. But as the Mothers' awaken, so too will my power rise. There is a caveat to this, a small way around our connection."

"My daughter," Heekah didn't ask, she knew that Kuin was somehow the key in B'nakma's plans.

"Indeed. Your daughter, when her powers awaken, if killed before she were to take the throne, would give me access to all of her magic. I can drain her, but not until she was awakened. So, I couldn't kill her as a babe, nor could I end the pathetic boy that once inhabited this body. I needed a body strong enough, the son of a warrior, and I needed your daughter to live long enough to awaken. Ideally, she would have awakened on earth, perhaps she would have been thrown into an insane asylum, but she would have been easy for me to drain. It would have taken nothing to end her simple little life if she didn't know the power she held."

"But now she does know. Now she has access to her power. She will destroy you, and you will never have the worship you so desperately crave," Heekah spat.

B'nakma laughed, a full, deep rumble. "She does indeed have her power. But she is untrained, and thanks to my tossing your husband and that simple little Wise over the side of a bridge, and you being stuck here with me, there are none to teach her. She may be able to get in a few blows, but she will not be able to kill me. Even if she had the strength, she could never do what needed to be done to end me as long as I inhabit this body," the god gestured the length of his form. "So, she will die, I will take her power as my own, and with that I will end the dragons once and for all."

Heekah wanted to weep, wanted to scream, wanted to twist and writhe, but she knew that she could not escape the clutches of the God of Darkness. He may not be at full power, but his power was far greater than hers. Perhaps had she not given up the throne, the magic of being queen would have been enough to at least make it a fair fight. But right now, there was nothing she could do. And so, she would allow B'nakma to think that he had won, she would go along for now, until the time came when she could do something to impact his plans.

As if reading her mind, the shadow of a smile crossed onto B'nakma's face. "Scheme as you will, oh great queen, but you can do nothing to stop what is coming. I will let you watch as it unfolds though. You can have a front row seat for the execution of your daughter, and the rise of my reign. I may even leave you alive long enough to watch as I eliminate the dragons, to watch as your bloodline is whittled down to only you, before silencing it for all of eternity."

Kuin stood, brushing off the grass from her pants. The horses that had run off at the excitement of the past few minutes had meandered back to them as she had wept. Enough tears had been shed.

"We need to get to Yilo. If we push, we will get there before the sun sets."

Gungdilkew stood and nodded. They wanted to say something, anything, to try to bring comfort to Kuin, but every time that they started to speak the words felt hollow. What could they possibly say to the princess to help her right now? No, they decided that the best way to help the princess was to stand by her side and be a reliable friend in a world of uncertainty.

The two rode without stopping until the very edges of the mountain range that surrounded Yilo appeared on the horizon, the orange of the setting sun beginning to wane.

They made it to the mountains as the last light of day seeped from the sky, darkness taking over. A path led to an archway that cut into the mountain. Two statues of a centaur rearing back on its strong legs, front legs kicking out, mirrored each other on either side of the narrow road. The road, if one could even call it that, was barely wide enough for the two companions to walk side by side, sheer walls of stone stretching up higher than they could see in the dim light of early night.

Gungdilkew took Kuin's hand as they left the horses behind. "I don't like this."

Kuin shook her head, though she doubted that they could see the movement in the dim light. "Me either, but we have no choice. This is where we are supposed to go, and there is nowhere to shelter until morning. We must hope that the centaur's are welcoming."

They walked in silence for another ten minutes or so before the tight path opened up and revealed wide open plains and what appeared to be a castle silhouetted in the young moonlight in the distance.

As soon as they got to the edge of the mountains, the stone walls that they had been walking between coming to an end, an arrow thudded into the ground at each of their feet. Instinctively they both put their hands up to show they were not a threat.

"We've come looking for an audience with the leader of the clans," Gungdilkew said, their voice holding firm and carrying into the night.

"Who are you," a voice answered back.

"I am Gungdilkew of the tree fairies. This," they said with a gesture to Kuin, "is Princess Kuin, First of her name, Daughter of Heekah, and Granddaughter of Gwimsum."

Hooves clacked on the path behind them, and two large centaurs stepped out, one from either side of the cliff walls. They were surrounded by four centaurs, two blocking the path back, and two guarding the path forward.

One of the creatures that stood before them stepped closer. His coat was black and shiny, and Kuin thought of the movie 'Black Beauty' that she had watched at the Palace Theatre what felt like a lifetime ago. But unlike the horse in the movie, this majestic creature had the strong, muscular torso of a man, his face chiseled with a short cut beard wrapping around it.

"I am Trabyu, General to Chieftain Hyod. You are hunted, Kuin the First, and you would bring this danger to our home?"

Gungdilkew opened their mouth like they intended to say something, but Kuin answered before they could. "We come to seek friendship and unification. Our reason for coming to your home is in no way to bring danger."

Trabyu made a loud cry that sounded like words, but nothing that resembled Hilchan. The other centaurs all took position beside him. "Follow us."

37

The four led Kuin and Gungdilkew toward their city, the form of their castle visible in the distance; the darkness made it difficult to see more than the shape and size of it, but what they could see was certainly majestic. A spire rose several stories into the air on all four corners of the building, dark stone with flickering lights in windows. As they approached the portcullis that led into the city, the four centaur split into groups of two on either side of them.

"Wait," Trabyu said, holding up a hand.

Again, he spoke in a language that Kuin couldn't understand, and the portcullis rose near silently save for the small rumble of the steel gate against the stone of the castle.

"You will be taken to the feasting hall. Chieftain Hyod will offer you food and drink, if you do not accept you will offend him greatly and I can assure you, you do not want to offend him. After you have eaten, he will meet with you briefly and you will be given accommodations for the night. Tomorrow, he will decide if he wishes to unify with you or not."

As they walked through the city toward the castle, it was clear that the day was winding down around them. Folks packed up their stalls in the market, closing them down for the night. Many seemed to head for taverns, while others presumably went to their homes. Kuin looked around in awe at the city. It looked like she would expect a medieval city to look, with one exception.

"Everything is so," Kuin paused, finding the right word, "wide."

Trabyu snorted, though whether it was a laugh or out of derision, Kuin couldn't be sure. "Perhaps you hadn't noticed, human," the creature almost spat the word, "but we are longer than you. We need space to turn around."

Kuin and Gungdilkew followed silently the rest of the way, winding the wide roads through the city, past the scowls of the fifty or so centaurs that they passed.

The majesty of her surroundings drew Kuin in. No centaur that they passed stood less than seven feet tall, and she knew that even the oldest of them held more strength than even the strongest human. Occasionally one of them would spit on the ground and curse them as they walked by. Kuin was coming to realize that humans were universally hated in Hilcha.

"Stop," Trabyu said, snapping Kuin from her thoughts.

The group came to a halt before the castle, its mighty doors open, the sounds of revelry and the smell of cooked meats wafting out towards them.

A guard stood on either side of the doors, and in the center a centaur stood announcing every group as they entered. The herald looked disdainfully at Kuin and Gungdilkew as they approached. Without a word, he turned and stood at the edge of the door.

"Trabyu and his Majesty's guards, escorting Kuin the Human and Gungdilkew the fairy."

The crowd inside fell silent. The herald moved to the side, and Kuin and Gungdilkew were ushered into the castle.

A foyer of polished stone, with a ceiling two stories high, led into a dining hall. The hall had to be at least twice as big as the theatre that Kuin once lived above.

The four corners of the room boasted pillars of fluted white marble. Kuin followed the length of the pillars, easily fifty feet tall. Supported by the pillars was a domed ceiling, and upon the ceiling was painted a great mural.

The outside of the mural was every sort of mythical creature Kuin could imagine. No, not mythical, Kuin realized, just every sort of creature from Hilcha. Fighting side by side with the centaurs were dragons, fairies, trolls, and what looked like giants. In the waters, mers fired arrows at dark figures, demons and shades of B'nakma. As the mural got closer to the center, the dark figures became more and those fighting them became less.

The mers no longer appeared in the waters and the dragons did not burn from the skies. The trolls and giants were also absent from the interior half of the mural, and the races that remained became segregated, each fighting with their own kind, no longer side by side. At the very center of the mural, a dark, wispy figure of smoke stood with the bodies of every race lying dead around them.

"Magnificent, is it not," a deep voice echoed through the room, breaking the silence and drawing Kuin's attention from the mural.

A centaur strode forward toward them, a crown sitting crooked on his head. A crisp, cream colored jacket with golden buttons perfectly accented his rich olive skin and chestnut coat. He held a glistening silver mug in his hand.

"It is, though I think it tells a sad story," Kuin answered, bowing her head respectfully, but not kneeling.

"It tells history. Dragon's and all races standing against darkness, before bigotry and distrust split us apart. We pushed the so called 'god' back and back, further away from the heart of our land before he was imprisoned on his island at the top of the world."

"We," Kuin asked, raising a single eyebrow.

"Aye," the centaur answered, taking a large swig of the contents of his tankard. "We, the centaurs, as everyone knows but no one outside of this kingdom acknowledges."

Kuin looked back up at the mural. "And what of the others that are fighting as well?"

The creature roared with a full, deep laugh. "The others? They may have killed some of B'nakma's demons, or perhaps some of those who chose to side with him, but we, the centaurs, and particularly those of us who were part of the Kni Wingwo, are the ones that pushed B'nakma into his prison."

The centaur looked at Kuin for a moment. "But, certainly that is not a tale to be told over dinner. Forgive my terrible manners, I am Hyod, second of my name, chieftain of the centaurs, lord of Yilo. Welcome, Kuin."

The chieftain's lack of acknowledgment of Gungdilkew, as well as the fact that he did not use her title, caused Kuin to bristle, but she held her tongue.

"Please," Hyod continued, "enjoy our dining hall and feast with us. It has been many years since a human has graced these walls."

Kuin and Gungdilkew were ushered to a table directly in front of the chieftain's. The main table where Hyod sat with Trabyu and a host of others was a step above everyone else's. The only two chairs in the hall were set for herself and Gungdilkew. To Hyod's left sat a beautiful female, her ebony coat shined in the light of the candles and lamps that burned around them. From the waist up, Kuin thought she could be a model back on earth. Her hair on her head was fire red, a contrast to her coat. Her heart shaped face smiled softly at Kuin, and her head dipped in a respectful nod. Kuin didn't know how long centaurs lived, but the female looked closer to her age than to Hyod's.

In front of the table that Kuin and Gungdilkew were sat at, a semi-circle of tables went around the room, leaving an open half-moon space of polished stone between the majority of those present and their table.

Hyod stood. "Tonight, we have guests," he addressed the crowd. "We shall eat and drink with our guests, we shall show them the warm hospitality of Yilo, and tomorrow we will perhaps become allies. Everyone, enjoy this historic night, eat, drink, and dance!"

Those gathered cheered and banged their cups on the tables. Music began playing from a balcony above them. Kuin had been so awed by the mural that she hadn't noticed the band that was positioned high above them. Kuin realized that it wasn't a band, as much as it was a drumline. Bass began shaking the tables as the drums played a fast rhythm and the sound reverberated off of the walls of the dining hall. Kuin wondered if it shook the entire castle. It wasn't long before the crowd began dancing, though Kuin thought it was more moshing than dancing.

The centaurs slammed into each other, and their hooves clacked off of the stone floor, mixing with the drums and creating a deafening cacophony. Kuin sat there and watched the spectacle. She felt Gungdilkew's hand take hers, their fingers twining together. She looked at them and they smiled.

"Not what I would plan for a fun night out, but if we were courting, would this be our first date," they leaned in and asked, their lips brushing her ear.

Kuin thought about it. As far as dates go, dinner with a tree fairy as the guests of a centaur chieftain whose tribe undulated to the sounds of drums was certainly not what Kuin would have ever imagined her first date being. But then again, Kuin would have never imagined that centaurs and fairies were real. She decided to embrace the moment.

Kuin stood, holding on to Gungdilkew's hand, she raised them up and stepped into them. "Dance with me?"

The fairy let the princesses' hand go and wrapped their arms around her waist, pulling her close to them. "I will dance with you anytime, anywhere," they whispered in her ear as she wrapped her arms around their neck.

The world around her faded into the background, and for the rest of the evening the princess and the fairy danced as if no one else existed.

When the drums stopped, and the crowd began to thin, Trabyu approached Kuin and Gungdilkew.

"Chieftain Hyod had matters to attend to. He has asked that I show you to your rooms for the evening."

Kuin reluctantly let Gungdilkew's body separate from hers. "Thank you," she said, and gestured for the guard to lead the way.

They were led out of the dining hall, and down a long, wide hallway. Paintings and sculptures of centaurs lined the walls. The end of the hall opened into an intersection, straight across was a wide, curved marble staircase. At the top, there was a small balcony with a door on either end.

"Both rooms are the same, they are two of our best rooms, reserved for dignitaries from other tribes or kingdoms. It has been many years since a human, or a fairy, has graced them, but I'm sure that you will find them comfortable. If there is anything that you need, there will be a servant posted at the bottom of the stairs to assist with any requests."

Kuin nodded and thanked the beast, though she couldn't help but think that the 'servant' at the base of the stairs was more like a guard to keep them from wandering.

She went into the room on the right, and Gungdilkew reluctantly went into the other room.

The room had a large bed, four posts covered with a soft linen canopy. A sitting area held a couch and a chair, and next to the bed was a soft, round mattress on the floor, presumably for centaurian guests.

Kuin was exhausted, and she was delighted to see that there was a bathtub and a fire for heating water. She drew herself a bath and slipped into the water. The heat loosened her muscles and she felt herself relax.

She thought about everything that had happened since leaving her parents' farm in Dwer. She had discovered her power, burned her friends, healed her friends, lost her father at the hands of a dark god, allied with, if not made friends with, Queen Feni and Queen Brimda, and watched her mother be taken by one of the dark god's demons. Tomorrow, she would try to convince Hyod, Chieftain of Yilo, to join her as well. When did she get to mourn? To let herself feel all of the emotions that she had burying just so that she could keep going around Hilcha to try to unite kingdoms that hate, or at the very least distrust, each other deeply, to join her and fight against a common enemy. Not tonight, not tomorrow, not next week, probably not next month, and likely not even next year.

The hot water warred with her emotions, trying desperately to keep her muscles loose as her emotion fought to keep her tense. She gave in, letting her emotions out. She wanted it to be a trickle, like turning on just a little bit of water from the tap, but once she let a little bit go, it rushed out of her like a waterfall.

Kuin sat in the tub and wept, sobbing loudly, allowing her tears and snot to run freely into her bath. Not knowing, nor caring, if anyone could hear her outside of the thick stone walls, she wept.

38

Kuin had sat in her bath so long, her fingers and toes wrinkled quite deeply, that by the time she stepped out the water was cold.

She had stopped crying long before she finally stood from the bath, splashing water on her face once before she did to take away the crusty streaks left behind in her tears wake. She dried off and wrapped her hair in the towel. She put on her rings and one of the oversize shirts that were in the wardrobe in her room, great for guests of a centaur build she was sure, but not great for a small, human girl. The shirt hung just past her knees, and the sleeves swallowed up her arm by half again the length she needed.

"Just a moment," she called out when there was a soft knock on her door, fastening the last button on the makeshift nightgown.

She opened the door to see Gungdilkew standing there. "I thought perhaps you would like some company."

Kuin stepped aside and let them in. "Could you hear me through the walls?"

They smiled softly at her. "Not much. But I know things have been moving very fast, and I know that you have been very strong. Everyone deserves a moment to stop and let their emotions settle in. If you'd prefer to be alone, I understand."

Kuin closed the door. "No, please, come in."

Gungdilkew sat on the couch, Kuin sat down next to them and rested her head on their shoulder. "Thank you," she said quietly.

They laid their head on top of hers and took her hand. "No need to thank, I was feeling a bit lonely myself."

They felt Kuin shake her head. "Not just for the company. Thank you for being my friend, thank you for standing by me, even after I've screwed things up and made mistakes."

Gungdilkew squeezed her hand. "We all make mistakes. Why don't you tell me about Graystone?"

Kuin knew that they were changing the subject, but she was happy to talk about her brother. So many things were happening, and sometimes she almost forgot why she was doing all of this. It had become about defeating B'nakma, and somehow the dark god had turned into a faceless threat. Kuin wondered if her mind was purposefully trying to block out the fact that B'nakma shared a face, a body, with Graystone. It was easier to think about defeating a dark god than it was to think about having to battle an enemy that looked like the brother she loved.

Kuin laid her head in their lap and looked up at the fairy. She spent the next few minutes telling the fairy stories about her brother, times he had saved her, times he had annoyed her, times that he had made her feel like she finally had someone in the world to call family, d'nu. Soon, Kuin was getting tired, the exhaustion once again catching up to her.

"Will you stay," she asked after another yawn.

Gungdilkew shook their head. "No, I think that for the sake of your reputation, it would be best if I don't. Regardless of the fact that I want to sleep next to you, and regardless of the fact that we would know that we had done nothing wrong, your image as the Princess of Hilcha would be better served by me sleeping in my own bed."

Kuin sat up with a smile and touched their cheek. "And if I say I don't give a damn about my image?"

"I would say that you should, we need the kingdoms on your side if we wish to unite them all."

Kuin kissed them then. Butterflies erupted in her stomach, and she pulled back to look them in the eyes before kissing them again.

"Then I guess you should go," she said, finally pulling away from the fairy and touching their cheek once more.

Kuin walked them to the door, and the fairy kissed her one more time before she closed the door and rested her head on it. She smiled to herself. She had never had time for boys in Lorain. And now, it wasn't a boy at all, but a fairy that stole her heart and made her feel more special than she ever had.

As Kuin wrapped herself in the thick, soft blanket on the bed, she fell asleep wondering what it would be like to show Gungdilkew her world, the place that she grew up. She imagined holding their hand as she walked with them down Lakeview Beach as the sun set on a summer day, the Mile Long Pier as the sun came up on a cool morning, and the Palace Theatre where she had spent so much of the last couple of years. If Bo had been able to appear human for all those years, surely there was a way for a tree fairy to blend in on earth for a few days. A smile graced her face as she fell asleep thinking about what the future might hold.

39

Kuin was awakened to the sound of shouting. She sat up in bed, and tried to make sense of what she was hearing. She thought she heard Gungdilkew yelling something, but just as she swung her feet off of the bed the door crashed in. Trabyu grabbed her and tossed her roughly to another guard.

"What are you doing," Kuin practically shrieked, heat rising in her core before she even realized it.

"The cuffs, now," Trabyu said to one of the guards still in the doorway.

The guard came and put cold shackles on Kuin's wrists, and she felt her power, the heat that had started to burn, disappear instantly.

"What did you do," she asked as she reached inward for her fire. She felt nothing.

"The magic that the fairies had used to try to subdue you was an early attempt at what we have imbued those cuffs with. We sold them the spells, but we gave them ones that we knew would not withstand someone of your power."

Kuin shook her head, trying to clear it. "How do you know what happened in Dispok?"

"The God B'nakma has spies everywhere," Trabyu smiled. "He needs you, but he does not need him."

Kuin looked to where Trabyu gestured. "Them," she corrected when she saw Gungdilkew, bound and gagged but struggling against his chains.

Trabyu ignored her correction. "Your companion will be held in the dungeon until we can arrange some sort of bargain with Queen Feni. If she doesn't choose to save him, then we will burn him," the centaur said with a careless pop of his shoulders.

"The Mothers will not allow this," Kuin said with far more confidence than she felt.

Trabyu laughed and glanced to one of the other guards. "Do you hear this little human?"

The other guard laughed and shook his head as Trabyu backhanded Kuin, knocking her down.

Trabyu knelt down, his front legs bending in what almost resembled a bow. He grabbed Kuin by the arm and pulled her close. "The Mothers aren't going to do anything. Only one has been able to muster the strength to even fly, and they won't return to full strength until B'nakma does. And what good, I can't help but wonder, is a dragon against a God?"

The centaur stood and dragged Kuin up to her feet, tossing her back to one of the other guards. "Take them to the dungeons."

Gungdilkew had struggled even more when they saw Kuin with blood running down her chin from where she had been struck. Their struggle ended when one of the guards drew his sword and struck the fairy in the back of the head with the pommel. The sound, like wood splintering, sickened Kuin as she watched her friend go limp.

One of the guards dragged the fairy's limp body by their arms, their green sap-blood slowly dripping to the ground from the back of their head, leaving a streak as their feet dragged through it.

"I will kill all of you," Kuin said, anger, but still no fire, flashing in her eyes. "I will burn every single centaur in this castle, and then I will bring the castle down, leaving your carcasses buried in a pile of stone, a mass grave for everyone that stood against us."

The guard holding her arm kicked her legs out from under her, pain making her see stars as the guard switched his grip to the shackles and began dragging her too.

Kuin let out a flurry of curses, simply causing the guard to laugh that much more. "Settle down, puny human. The God has demanded that you be delivered, but there is nothing that requires you to be delivered with your bones intact."

The two guards dragged them down a set of stairs, Gungdilkew finally waking up as their feet bounced down the steps behind them. To their credit, the fairy didn't struggle. They looked at Kuin, and she shook her head. Now was not the time for conversation or explanation.

At the bottom of the stairs, they were dragged out of a door and into the star-filled night. They were dragged along a cobblestone path the length of the castle. In the distance, Kuin could hear water lapping at stone, and a salty breeze confirmed that they were by the sea. She mentally chided herself for not learning more of the Hilcha's geography.

"Time to see your new rooms," the one holding Kuin said with a laugh.

Fear and panic bubbled up in Kuin, and though she tried she couldn't stop herself from again fighting against the centaur. She slipped his grip and kicked his thin leg as hard as she could. She had learned long ago that horses had weak legs and often had to be put down when they broke. She hoped that the same was true for the centaur.

Her swift kick was rewarded with the snap of bone, and the painful howl as the creature crumpled in pain. The other guard stood above Kuin and reared up on his hind legs. Time seemed to slow as two solid hooves and two thousand pounds hung in the air, ready to strike down onto Kuin.

Kuin tried to will herself to move, to get out of the way, but she was frozen in fear. She promised herself that if she survived, she would never let fear paralyze her again. But that promise did nothing to help her now.

Before the legs could come down on top of Kuin, a flash of steel pierced the side of the centaur, pushing it off course. The ground vibrated as the beast landed beside her, dead eyes staring into starlight.

Kuin looked to where the sword had come from, just in time to see Trabyu spin and slice his sword through the neck of the other guard. After she broke his leg, the guard had sat and groaned. Now the cursing and sounds of pain stopped, and his head rolled down the red stained cobblestone path.

Kuin scampered back and away from Trabyu, who wiped his sword on the side of the first centaur before sheathing it once again. "You don't need to fear me," he said.

Reaching down, he released the shackles from Gungdilkew. He turned to Kuin. "I am going to remove your chains, but I need you to not barbecue me."

Kuin raised an eyebrow. "There is barbecue in Hilcha?"

Trabyu opened his mouth to respond but closed it. Shouting and the sound of galloping hooves was coming from the far end of the path.

"Run," Trabyu said. "Run and don't stop, you are going to have to jump at the end. But it is better than staying here."

Kuin leapt to her feet. When she started to ask Trabyu what the hell was going on, an arrow ricocheted off of the wall to her right. "There's no time," the centaur snarled. "Run, and don't stop."

Gungdilkew grabbed Kuin's arm and started running. Kuin didn't resist and together they ran towards the sounds of the sea. In the moonlight, all Kuin could see was open field before them. Her hands still bound in shackles, her lack of power left her feeling hollow. Arrows thudded into the grass on either side of them as they ran.

Kuin screamed in pain, as one of the arrows bit into the flesh of her calf. She fell and was immediately picked up by Gungdilkew, the fairies limbs carrying her with ease as the arrows continued to land around them.

The sound of the lapping water got louder, the salty air thicker, until, with a series of curses, Gungdilkew came to a sudden stop.

"What," Kuin asked, twisting in their arms to see what was before them.

When she saw what caused Gungdilkew to pause, she too joined in their curses. They stood at a cliffs edge. Behind them, the sound of hooves got louder, the ground seeming to shake with the beating of them. Arrows whistled as they soared past them.

"We have to jump," Gungdilkew said, glancing over the edge. The drop was at least a hundred feet.

"We'll die! I can't swim with my hands bound," Kuin said, panic again taking her over.

"And I can't swim at all. But, nonetheless, we have-".

Whatever else the fairy was going to say was stopped short by the arrow that pierced their chest, just missing where they held Kuin. They looked at her, sadness and fear filling their eyes as the two of them tumbled off of the cliff and into the water below.

Rage filled B'nakma as he watched the scene from his study. Anger burned him as he watched the cowardly centaur free the princess and her friend, watched as they fell over the edge of the cliff. Pure, uncontrolled fury caused him to scream in rage as he watched clawed hands latch on to the two bodies in the water and pull them down, down, down, into the darkness of the ice-cold waters.

Epilogue

Kuin awoke in a bed, warm soft, lush blankets covering her, her head resting upon a soft pillow. There were no walls around her, simply posts that held up sheer linen around the room. A muted, bluish light filtered into the room and she could hear the soft sounds of water on a beach outside.

She sat straight up in bed when she remembered the cliffs in Yilo that they had jumped from. No, she realized, they hadn't jumped. Gungdilkew had been shot through with an arrow and they fell.

She looked down at her wrists, ecstatic to see that they were no longer bound. She could feel the tingle of her power, a consistent and comforting thrum. She practically jumped out of the bed and pulled aside the linen covering the room.

As soon as she exited, she stopped in her tracks. She was at the base of a great hill, buildings carved into the side all the way up. At the top, a shining white palace sat regally. She could not see the sky, but rather what looked like pure darkness past the blue tinted light of the city before her.

There was a sand path from where her room was to a cluster of buildings a few hundred feet away. As she got closer to the buildings, she felt the dizzying feeling that she had somehow been transported not only back to earth, but back in time. The structures were clearly Grecian in their design, and the path to them was lined with statues of

Greek gods, some of whom she could clearly identify, some she wasn't sure of. At the end of the path, directly before it changed from sand to polished stone, stood a twenty-foot-tall marble statue of Poseidon.

In the dull, bluish glow that surrounded her, the marble seemed to almost move, giving the illusion of it being not entirely solid. In his right hand, the Greek god held a trident of pure, shining gold.

For a moment, Kuin forgot herself. Forgot Gungdilkew, forgot Hilcha, forgot everything she knew and was drawn into the magic of it.

The spell was broken by three simple words, spoken by a voice behind her. A voice she never thought she would hear again, a voice that brought everything that she had gone through in Hilcha back in an instant. "Hello, my sunshine."

www.ingramcontent.com/pod-product-compliance
Lightning Source LLC
Chambersburg PA
CBHW010401310726
48979CB00017B/2813/J